ALASKAN ESCAPE

ALASKAN WOMEN OF CALIBER SERIES

MARYANN LANDERS

Copyright © 2022 by Maryann Landers

All rights reserved.

No part of this book may be reproduced in any form or by any electronic or mechanical means, including information storage and retrieval systems, without written permission from the author, except for the use of brief quotations in a book review.

All scripture quotations are taken from the Holy Bible, King James Version, KJV, public domain.

Book Cover Design: Pro_ebookcovers, Fiverr

Editors: Jessica Martinez Copywriting and Editing Services and Kameo Monson Editing Services

Map and Anchor Drawing by Sonya Bitz

❦ Created with Vellum

Dedicated to my friend Colleen who has shared her testimony of God's grace and peace during the storms of her life. You shine the truths of His Word.

ENDORSEMENTS

"A delightful and thought-provoking story of a woman weathering the storms of life and learning to trust in God's grace. Don't miss *Alaskan Escape*."
—Darlene L. Turner, best-selling and award-winning author

CONTENTS

Foreword	xi
Preface	xiii
Chapter 1	1
Chapter 2	11
Chapter 3	18
Chapter 4	25
Chapter 5	34
Chapter 6	43
Chapter 7	50
Chapter 8	57
Chapter 9	63
Chapter 10	69
Chapter 11	75
Chapter 12	81
Chapter 13	89
Chapter 14	99
Chapter 15	108
Chapter 16	115
Chapter 17	121
Chapter 18	129
Chapter 19	136
Chapter 20	140
Chapter 21	147
Chapter 22	153
Chapter 23	159
Chapter 24	165
Chapter 25	172
Epilogue	178
Acknowledgments	187
About the Author	189
Also by Maryann Landers	191

FOREWORD

Thank you to my launch team for *Alaskan Escape*. Your time, attention to detail and enthusiasm for this story are all appreciated.

Phylis Carpenter
- Heather Deeter
- Marsha Woodrum
- Toni Stevens
- Cheryl Wood
- Gretchen Garrison
- Heather Sample
- Mara Mittleman
- Mrs. Brent Magers
- Shelly Sulfridge
- Eden Clark
- Sheree Fournerat
- Ginger Skaggs
- Mary McCauley

PREFACE

This story was based on actual events except of course when they didn't happen and the people didn't exist. I muddled the time frame and changed elements for dramatic purposes.

There weren't any real or imagined boats damaged in the creation of this novel. Nor were any shrimp or fish wasted in the efforts of developing the plot.

Also, Wrangell, Alaska is a real and fascinating city in Southeast Alaska. If you ever get the chance to visit- Take it! It was home for me and my family for two years and the amazing experience will stay with me a lifetime.

CHAPTER 1

I WATCHED MY HUSBAND CROUCH IN PLACE, AWAITING the release of the black panther. The cat's emerald eyes escalated the tension on the movie set. Bill pursed his lips, and I mimicked his rhythmic breathing. After twenty-three years of marriage, I was in tune with his every move and could read even the slightest twitch. As he watched the caged animal with intense focus, I was assured he was comfortable in his role.

Together, we'd committed to acting in movies using trained but otherwise wild animals like grizzlies, snakes, and panthers. I checked my watch and noted that we had one more scene, which allowed us time to arrive home and make supper for our five kids.

We'd practiced our parts with precision and repetition, and in a moment, the predator would release at the sound of the buzzer as it had countless times before.

To the right of the set, a cage contained the long body of the panther, whose black fur shimmered in the low light. His muscular legs stalked his cage. I appreciated the intelligence of the cat and how it was trained to behave as a fierce predator through the use of small fish snacks hidden from the camera. It was all part of the show, leading an audience to believe the animal was lethally bursting onto stage, savagely seeking its human prey. The appearance was all that mattered; the graceful beast was only a crew member acting its part.

C'mon, let's finish this.

There was comfort in the knowledge that the animals were trained, but tension lingered at the end of the long day, taking its toll on my thoughts. Offstage, I crossed my legs and shifted my position on the stool. Danger lurking in every scene was supposed to be a casual happenstance. But I recalled how my heart had raced with worry a few weeks ago when a bear reverted to its natural instinct and clawed at me. That night, I'd spoken to Bill about my doubts over continuing with the acting crew. He'd used statistics to assure me I would more likely die in a car accident. His calm promisee of the expert training that was carried out on and off set temporarily calmed my nerves.

The Brazilian animal trainer assumed the director's role during the animal scenes, and he picked up his loudspeaker. "Alright, you're set, Bill. I'll count it down from three." He scanned the crew of actors and stagehands, including myself, and nodded in our direction.

I closed my eyes and breathed a prayer for safety. Then I opened my eyes, setting my gaze on my man, strong and muscular from years of working on the family farm. I never voiced a fear with him nearby since I felt shielded in a cocoon when I was with him. His presence was commanding and protective even though he was a gentle giant—well over six feet tall.

In this career, we learned to juggle the instinct to flee and played along with beasts.

The fan blew the potted palm trees, creating a space similar to the Brazilian jungle the panther called home. Above the noise of the fans, the stereo speakers blared bird calls and trickling water. The Brazilian animal trainer, Bruno, called out, "three, two, and one."

Chapter 1

The Pavlovian buzzer sounded, and the cage gate was lifted by two stagehands. Franz, a heavyset man who'd worked for decades with the crew, helped loosen the gate. As he pulled it, the panther swiped at the bars, and Franz threw the gate into the air, sending it sailing toward Bill where it clanged on the floor beside him.

In a trance-like prowl, the panther moved gracefully toward the obscured fresh-fish snack he knew was his promised prize. His piercing eyes squinted, and his nose sniffed the air.

The practiced pattern was for the feline to walk past Bill and feed on its treat beyond, where it remained.

Instead, the panther froze. Its nose twitched and eyes darted. What did it sense? Why didn't it move forward? Turning, the panther stared menacingly at Bill.

I gasped and covered my mouth. *Dear Lord, help us!* I prayed.

Bruno sprang into action, running to Bill and yelling out commands in Portuguese as he drew a long knife from its scabbard.

Bill rolled off his perch on a rock and fell to the left. He grabbed the cage gate, which had landed within reach moments before, and guarded his face with it. The panther leaped toward him, snarling and revealing long claws that swiped at the metal.

I felt light-headed as I held my breath and gripped the stool that I sat on with both hands.

Bruno grasped the animal around its neck, pulled it from the cage gate, and held a long knife to its throat as he snarled out commands.

Bill crumbled and panted, sweat pouring off his face. He raised his head and looked to me with tears in his eyes. Our worst fear had come true. Bill was the victim of an attack from the enemy.

I searched the set, unsure whether it was safe to move toward him. Frozen with fear I willed myself to get up, but I couldn't. Would the panther rebel against Bruno? My heart still racing, I raised my hand to my chest and shook my head, blinking watery eyes.

Inching forward, Bill came to me and pulled me up. He engulfed me in his burly arms with his damp shirt against my cheek and squeezed me fiercely.

"I'm sorry, Grace," he whispered.

I pulled back and looked up. "Don't be sorry."

"You mentioned your fears…" He panted, catching his breath. "I've had mine too. We're done here."

Bill was an exemplary provider for our growing family and almost ten years older than me. We'd farmed together and then worked alongside one another on set when the opportunity came knocking a few years ago.

"Babe? What will we do?" I asked, searching his deep blue eyes. The same eyes that'd first lured me to him the day I saw him casually watching me roller skate past him as I carried a tray full of hamburgers and drinks.

Bill loosened his grasp on me and turned to watch the crew harness and cage the panther. "I don't know," he said.

He walked over to Bruno and shook his hand. I heard their muffled voices and Bruno nodded.

Returning to me, Bill placed his hand on the small of my back. "He said we're done for the day." He rubbed my shoulders. "And I said we're done for good."

I gulped back the lump in my throat. There was no doubt in my mind we'd walk away, but what would we do? Our five kids were a strain on the money we earned.

"We'll have a debriefing tomorrow. Bruno asked us to come." Bill took my hand in his and pulled me over to the movie props, where we'd set our backpacks down earlier.

The urge to run out the gates of the ranch hand in hand with Bill took root, and I stared down at my feet. Another debriefing —why did we have to relive the terror of the day like we'd done with the bear? Wasn't it enough to admit mistakes were made?

Remembering the hurt only pulled open wounds, exposing the raw truth that we couldn't rely on others for our safety. Sometimes we had to regain what we'd lost on our own.

Be still.

The portion of a scripture verse came to mind, and I shook my head. *God, how do I be still?*

I placed my shaking hand on my forehead and tried to regain my thoughts. Bill touched my cheek with the palm of his hand, reassuring me of his presence.

"It's going to be okay." He handed my bag to me and pointed to the gate.

We moved past the main staging area on the ranch where the filming took place and went down the dirt road to where our Suburban was parked. As we walked, I pulled off the bandana I used as a headband and ran my hands through my shoulder-length blonde hair. I pulled at some of the tangles that had formed because of the forceful fans on set.

"Want to hear a wild idea?" Bill asked.

"Sure." I pulled out the hooded sweatshirt I'd packed earlier.

"Alaska." Bill swung his bag over his wide shoulder.

"Alaska? Good land, where'd that come from?"

Bill had been my sweetheart since I was eighteen. I worked as a car hop at the local A &W, and he'd pulled in on his motor bike and eyed me from head to toe. He told me I was the cutest girl he'd ever seen and asked if I wanted to go for a ride sometime? That summer night, I vowed to follow him anywhere, and we'd been together ever since.

"I've mentioned how I've always wanted to go there. Wait'n on a good time to peel away I guess."

"Peel away? Bill, we've got five kiddos stacked into our home, along with three dogs. We've family here. What would we do in Alaska?"

Bill shrugged and sauntered next to me. How did he play off the attack and stride casually unscathed? I'd appreciated his recoil and determination over the years, but where did I fit into *this* dramatic turn of events?

Our large log home was nestled on fifteen acres, next to my mom's, where I visited regularly. She had me late in life, and I arrived at the end of a string of several children, all much older than myself. Now, they were busy with their families, and I cared for our eighty-year-old mom religiously, especially since I was her only child that shared her Christian faith.

"Baby, you worry too much." Bill drew me in, placing his arm around my shoulder. He placed a kiss on my head and pulled me close to walk in step with him.

We strode side by side, and I tried to yield to the sheltered and safe warmth of his embrace and the reassurance that we'd be okay and find somewhere to escape.

THE KIDS AND I SAT IN A SEMICIRCLE ON THE RUG near the woodstove. Our home was an oasis where I let down any wall built around broken memories or painful thoughts. It was here that I felt truly at peace with the day's events. Perhaps it was the children's laughter as we played a game of Clue and made accusations about *who done it*. Their joy was a balm to my soul.

Sitting crisscrossed with a hand of cards, I smiled at each of their faces. Stanna, Rob, Daniel, Laura, and Rayna. The brood I'd yearned and prayed for.

We'd suffered several long years of infertility before going to the elders of the church and pleading for divine intervention for conception. Persistent prayers and more waiting and then the flood gates opened. Now, our cup ran over in blessings of noise, dirty dishes, and piles of laundry.

Chapter 1

"Mom," Stanna questioned. "are you tired?"

At sixteen, Stanna was the oldest of the kids. She was intuitive and knew me well. I relied on her keen sense of timing and attention to detail.

"Sorry about that. Lost in thought. And yes, I'm tired."

I played my turn and grinned at Stanna, who raised an eyebrow. I was certain she'd noted the change in Bill's and my tone when we'd picked her and her siblings up from school. Now she lingered in her questions. I'd have to talk privately with her and fill her in on the details. I gave her a wink of reassurance.

Rayna leaned against me and yawned. "Momma, I'm going to bed."

I put my arm around her and gave her a side hug. "You sure? We haven't finished the game yet."

Because she was the youngest of the five, Rayna was always an early-morning riser. It wasn't uncommon for her to curl up on the couch while the rest of us played cards or told stories around the kitchen table.

"Alrighty, good night." I ruffled the top of her head and repositioned myself back against the couch.

She stood and meandered upstairs.

"I'll come tuck you in soon," I called after her.

"My turn," Rob stated, holding his cards in front of his face.

Rob was my second oldest, and my risk taker. He'd forge his way in this world, and we'd all need to stand back and watch him fly. At fourteen, he thought he was on top of the world, a young man wanting to try out his wings. *Lord, have mercy.* He'd take off on his own now if we'd let him. Bill and I had struggled to redirect his perseverance in his early years. I'd determined to view it positively, not as plain stubbornness.

"I'm going to make a guess." He thumbed his cards and coyly scanned our faces. "I think it's Mr. Green, in the conservatory, with a candlestick." He straightened his back and crossed his arms.

Laura reached for the envelope with the correct clues and slowly pulled the tab back. She knew how to ruffle her brother's feathers.

I smiled at her shenanigans and the variety of personalities in our family. Stanna was responsible, Rob was persistent, Daniel was quiet and consistent, Laura was playful and adventurous, and Rayna was our clown—and, as the youngest, with a few years between her and Laura, she was still finding her place in the family.

"Well, you have the character correct," Laura stated and paused. She was reeling Rob in.

"C'mon with it. Did I get it right?" Rob blurted and reached for the envelope that Laura drew closer to herself.

"Okay, okay, you were right. Game over," Laura announced.

Rob cheered, lifting his arms in the air.

Bill came into the living room from the adjacent kitchen and set his hand on Rob's shoulder. "Since you are a master sleuth, I'll leave you to figure out what needs to be done out in the barn, son."

Rob grunted. "Okay, Dad."

A smile spread across Bill's lips, and he nodded to me. "And what do you say we take our evening walk, my love?"

"I'll go," I answered. "Thanks for cleaning up the game guys."

Every evening, Bill and I would walk the perimeter of our property. It was our alone time to discuss the kids or anything else from the day that needed to be dealt with before the sun went down. I looked forward to our time together and would often keep a list on the counter of items I wanted to remember to tell him, even if it was about a postcard that came in the mail or something one of the kids may have said that was funny. We shared a friendship I knew many couples didn't. We had endured hard times over the years, but thankfully, our faith in

God helped us form healthy convictions and practices. I believed meeting daily during our walks was one of them. And the fresh fall air and fragrance of the change of season were an added blessing this evening.

Outside, I sat on the front step and tied my tennis shoes. Did Bill have more to say about earlier? Was Alaska still at the front of his mind, or had he thought of something else to share? After he'd thrown the idea to me, I'd struggled to set it aside. Leaving home, even temporarily, sounded like running a marathon. There would be so much to do to transplant our home-grown family.

Bill's cheery humming announced his arrival through the front door, and he came down the steps and reached his hand out to help me up. I grasped it and pulled him close. "Whoa, there baby." He teased.

I squeezed his hand and looked up to his tanned face. "I love our walks."

"I do too." We held hands in silence as we traveled further from the house and over to a fence that lined our property. Along it grew a row of trees we'd planted when we'd first built our home. With each child, we planted a new one. The joy of watching the trees grow from saplings was similar to watching the kids mature in their stature and spiritual walk with the Lord.

"I made a couple of calls while you were playing your game with the kids." He squeezed my hand. "You know Steve lives in Wrangell, Alaska. He's heard of boat that's for lease."

I stared at my feet as I gulped. I'd forgotten about the close connection Bill had to Alaska through his brother. Perhaps he'd helped fuel his interest?

Bill continued. "Here's the thing. We can go up, fish the openers for shrimp, continue on for the spring crabbing season, and see what we think."

I turned to look at him. "We're a team, and I still don't know anything about those things. I guess I didn't study your resume well enough the day we met. When did you commercial fish?" I hoped my teasing would show I wanted to work alongside him, but I was clueless as to what that looked like.

Bill laughed and swung my hand. "Funny, I haven't. However, it sounds like it would be a simple and satisfying way for us to make some money and have family time all at once. Especially since we'd live on the boat."

I repeated his words, astonished. "Live, on the boat? Bill! We'd drive each other crazy." I enjoyed time with people, but as an introvert, I needed the quiet reprieve I scheduled into my days to regroup and refresh my thoughts.

We walked past the last tree and made a turn to the left to follow the rock garden along the front of our property. Rocks carefully placed as memorial stones were a project I'd done with the kids. Together, we'd painted them and drawn words of promise on top in remembrance of God's work in our lives. Like in the Old Testament.

Bill stopped and took my other hand in his as he faced me. "Let's pray about it. I won't mention it to the kids. How about in one week we come back before these memorial stones and see where God has led us?"

"I can do that," I answered. And I could. In another week certainly something else would rise to the surface. We'd be one more week into the busyness of fall and helping family with harvest. Yes, in seven days Alaska would be a memory, and we'd be rushing forward in our next adventure.

CHAPTER 2

THE KIDS JUMPED ON THE TRAMPOLINE PLAYING WITH their cousins from Bill's side of the family. They raced over to the adjacent lot where I sat on the porch swing with my mom. "I love watchin' 'em play," she said with a smile spread across her face. "Such a blessin' to have family close by." She reached out and placed her hand on top of mine.

"Aw, and we love being close to you, Momma." The breeze blew off the fields beyond our lots, and I closed my eyes.

This has always been my home. We'd built our log house next to my mom's place, and Bill's folks originally lived a couple of roads to the south. His parents moved after a few short years and relocated to a different part of the state. My elderly mom didn't often wander from home. We'd made it a weekly habit to have Sundays with her and invite other family to join us. Each week it was a different blend but there were always extras to feed ice cream to after dinner.

"What's on your mind, hun?" She rubbed my hand.

"Just watching the kids," I answered.

"No. You're stewin'. I can tell. Momma knows."

How could she tell? I'd aimed to mask any thoughts of

Alaska and keep them from my family. Until we knew the direction we were heading, the last thing I wanted was advice from over thirty people. The tug-of-war could be disastrous. I figured it was safe to say we were done with acting and leave it at that.

"We've decided to stop working on set, and we're praying about what's next. But I'm not worried. God will provide us with what we need." I pushed with my foot, moving the porch swing some more.

"Um-hm, then why the furrowed brow? You're not squintin'. It's okay if you don't want to tell me."

I'd told her a secret long ago that I held close. When I gathered the courage to share, she'd looked through me and I felt her doubt weigh me down like a rock floating to the bottom of a pond. I'd sunk out of sight. She'd believed the character of someone else over me. Perhaps my youthfulness as a teen made me appear naïve, but I'd seen what had happened, and I chose to tell her. In that instant, she let me tell her the whole story, but she didn't act on what I'd shared. How did I let that go, even now? Setting aside the fact that I felt betrayed, I said, "Not now. Bill and I are praying about doing something different for work that's all." I patted her arm and gave her a closed-mouth smile. I'd spoken the truth but hadn't told her everything. Wasn't that how it was when I was younger? Parts and pieces left undone?

"I'll be praying, baby girl. You know I will. I see somethin's a weighin' you down. God knows, and He will show the way." She sipped the tea she held in her hand. "He always does."

"These are good times, Momma, when we're all together like this." I rocked and watched the kids scrambling for a frisbee that had landed under the trampoline in our yard. They soon positioned themselves to send it flying over to their grandma's lawn.

"Have you been to see Amanda?" My mom asked about my friend from my childhood that'd recently moved back into the area. It was my mom who'd heard and told me how to find her.

"I've been meaning to. But no, I haven't."

"Oh, you should. I think it'd be good for your soul. Laugh a little together about your days spent like these youngins." She slapped her leg. "Oh, you two got some sweet memories to go over."

An image flashed through my mind of Amanda and me walking the path from town, singing at the top of our lungs early in the morning on the way to youth group. We didn't have a care in the world and were oblivious to the fact that folks might still be sleeping during the early morning hours. "You're right. We sure do. Thanks for the reminder. Maybe I'll do that this week." I stood and smoothed my shirt. "Can I help you with dessert? Might as well sugar up the kids so they can burn it off before bedtime."

My mom inched forward in her chair. "Baby girl? You've got some burning off to do of your own. I saw how you put back those home fries."

"Momma." I reached to help her stand, taking her hand. "You're relentless."

She pulled me in for a hug as we walked to the front screen door. "When you're my age. You can say whatever you want."

I opened the door for her and followed her into the home I'd grown up in. My dad left Earth in his mid-fifties. With my mom on her own, I was drawn near her and to give back to her as best I could. Convinced it was my duty as a daughter, I was willing to sacrifice my own wants to care for her. It wasn't begrudging, I was honored to serve her that way. Our relationship wasn't perfect. Was there a mother-daughter relationship that was seamless?

Following her into the kitchen, the aroma of the fresh baked cookies took me back to a time when I'd returned home from school as a teenager, and Momma sat reading her Bible. When I walked in, she looked up with tears in her eyes, and I'd hurried to her. She held onto me, thanking me for being an obedient child, thanking me for respecting her and honoring her. My older siblings were far away, not only in distance but also in their walk with the Lord. It must have been heavy on her heart that day. I didn't want to hurt her like that.

God, I don't want to leave Momma. Who will care for her? Who will be here when she needs me?

A verse immediately came to mind. *I will never leave you nor forsake you.*

God will be here for her, as He always had been.

Lord, I know. But who will be Your hands and feet?

The questioning prayer was not only for my mom, but me as well.

A WEEK AFTER OUR PANTHER INCIDENT, I WALKED along the front of our property, studying the memorial stones in our front yard. A group of rocks circled one of the trees. We'd colored all the rocks the same deep-blue hue. On them, we'd written the letters spelling out Psalm One.

Years ago, I strived to impress upon my growing kids with visual lessons they could relate to. Psalm One was a personal favorite that I'd hoped to pass along to them as a picture to follow. The Psalmist wrote of a tree being planted by the waters. Written as the prologue to the book of Psalms, the growth and protection we can have when we walk with God, delighting in Him and His word, stood out to me.

I looked back and forth along the road and behind me. There wasn't anyone in sight. "Alright, here it goes," I stated out loud. "I hope I can remember all the motions." Talking to myself, I straddled the grassy spot beneath my feet.

"Blessed is the man that walketh not in the counsel of the

ungodly"—I walked in place and then stood still—"nor standeth in the way of sinners."

I laughed out loud. "I hope no one sees me."

Continuing with the verses, I squatted as though on a chair. "Nor sitteth in the seat of the scornful." I toppled slightly and caught myself easing down to sit on the ground.

"But his delight is in the law of the Lord"—I opened my palms like opening a book—"and in his law doth he meditate day and night." Using sign language, I signed the word *day*.

As I eased up from the ground, I spread my arms out wide and spoke louder. "And he shall be like a tree planted by the rivers of water"—I reached out my hands and picked at the air —"that bringeth forth his fruit in his season." Shaking a finger, I resumed. "His leaf also shall not wither; and whatever he doth shall prosper." I reached my hands out in a straight line and pulled back one arm.

"The ungodly are not so"—I shook my finger and my head —"but are like the chaff which the wind driveth away." I pressed my arms to my sides.

"Therefore, the ungodly shall not stand in the judgment, nor sinners in the congregation of the righteous." I placed both arms at my sides, and stood tall with my shoulders back. "For the Lord knoweth the way of the righteous: but the way of the ungodly shall perish."

The memorization of verses from my youth came pouring to the front of my mind. Amanda and I had recited those verses over and over on our walks to Youth Time, laughing at our made-up hand motions. What had seemed silly at the time now triggered my recitations. I kneeled down and picked up the rock with the number one on it. "God, You are number one. Lead us to where You would have us so we can be like this tree planted firm and bring forth the fruit in our lives." In my own daydream world, I continued to squat and inspect the rocks, holding them in my hands and remembering how the kids had placed them with care and enthusiasm.

"Looking for a pet rock?" Bill questioned.

I turned and looked up at him peering down at me. I'd not heard him approach.

"Funny," I answered and stood up, putting my hands in my pockets. "I was waiting for my date."

"Oh? He's a lucky guy. Bill pulled me close for a hug and kissed the top of my head. "Because you're the cutest girl I've ever seen."

I loved being in his arms where he wrapped me in tight. "Yup, he's lucky alright." I teased back.

"I'm not just lucky, I'm blessed to have the most wonderful woman in the world who will, as she said, follow me *anywhere*."

There it was. We'd left the topic alone and promised to meet today, revisiting the thought of Alaska. "And?" I let the question hang in the afternoon air.

"And I can't let it go, babe. I can't shake it. Don't you think that *if* we shouldn't go that I'd be able to leave it alone? But I can't." His blue eyes searched mine.

"I don't know what to say because all week I tried *not* to think about it." I spurted the words out without considering whether it might hurt him. It was the truth though.

"We've got a lot of life ahead of us. Rayna's only five. There are years left for me to provide for all of you. I'm going to need your support, just like you've already given in our marriage. Can we give ourselves *one* season of fishing? Just the little ol' number one." He pinched his finger toward his thumb, leaving a small space between them.

The same number of the Psalm I'd just recited. Was it providential? I closed my eyes and breathed in a slow breath. "Yes, I can do one season. Together we can go and try this adventure and then return home to find something else."

Chapter 2

Bill pulled me close and squeezed me tight, holding my shoulders. "Babe, it's going to be great!"

I felt Bill's enthusiasm in his embrace, and he lifted me into the air and swung me around. As we swirled, my mind circled back to the concept of sailing away from the security of family and those we trusted for the unknown. On the outside, I smiled at Bill's enthusiasm, but inside I was kicking and screaming, *No, I don't want to go!*

CHAPTER 3

We walked the short path between our home and my mom's place in the quiet of the dark, mid-March evening. She'd invited us over for her cherry pie as a celebratory going-away before we left for Bellingham, Washington, the next morning. My kids walked ahead of me, the girls skipping and the boys racing to Grandma's. Bill would meet us at Mom's after he finished working on the leaky faucet in our kitchen.

Watching my steps in the low light, I asked myself how long it would be before I walked that way again?

"Wait for me," I called out to my eager crew, who'd left me trailing behind. Perhaps this was the picture of our move. Them racing ahead. Me, holding back enthusiasm and excitement. Me gripping onto what I loved in Oregon, instead of embracing the future.

I hurried my steps and caught up to my girls, and together, we walked into my mom's home. Stomping my feet on her entryway rug in, I called out, "Hey, Mom." I removed my coat and followed the boys' voices as they talked to her in the large kitchen ahead. They each sat on a stool eating nuts from a bowl.

Her eyes found mine, and she smiled while she listened to Rayna tell the story she'd saved for her about the special fishing pole she'd picked out. I'd explained to Rayna how our fishing wasn't going to be like she was used to—with a pole on the edge of a creek. We'd be out in deep waters, but she still didn't understand.

Rayna finished, and I jutted in. "Bill will be here after he fixes some plumbing. How've you been, Momma?" With all the tidying and packing over the last few weeks, I'd neglected my regular visits with her.

She shuffled to the counter by the stove and spoke as she moved. "Doing well, hun. Doing well." She placed some small plates on the counter in front of the boys and shook her finger at them. "Now don't forget to send me a postcard! I'll never forgive you if you do. I want to hear of all your adventures." That evening, my mom did well putting on a smile and mustering up some excitement to lather on the kids. Earlier in the month, when I'd confirmed our plans with her, the color had drained from her face.

"Here, you boys take these to the table, and we'll dish up the pie in a minute." She handed them some napkins. "Gracie"—pointing at me, she motioned with her hand—"you come with me."

I followed her into a small office that adjoined her kitchen. She shut the door and placed her hand over her heart. She inhaled deeply, then closed her eyes and opened them again. "I'm in no way tellin' you this isn't what you should do. But heaven knows when you go somewhere it might mean the end of what you leave behind." She waved her hand at me. "I'm not speaking of myself but of the relationship you have with the Lord. I've seen it before. My prayer for you and your family is that you will not grow away from Him."

I reached for my fragile mom, who stood bravely before me, and hugged her gently. "I'll do my best, Momma. And I know you'll be praying for us." I didn't tell her how afraid I was to leave or how I feared for her health and wondered who would step in to help her. I hugged her, knowing God was with her, and somehow, He would help us all. "I love you."

"I love you too, hun. My Gracie girl." She released me, wiped a tear from her eye, and pulled at the doorknob. "Now, let's go play some cards and whoop it up a bit."

I smiled at her and followed her back to the kitchen where my boisterous family waited to share some of Grandma's pie. I was certain it was made with, not only love, but a lot of prayer and petition.

"What do you say we dig in," she announced, picking up a spatula and waving it in the air.

My kids cheered, and I stood back watching them wait their turn for a slice of pie and an interaction with their grandma. We were about to leave it all behind us.

WE TRAVELED OVER THIRTY-SIX HOURS ON THE FERRY from Washington to Ketchikan and docked for a couple of hours. A few hours later, we'd left port en route to Wrangell with six hours between the two locations. The further north we went, the more briskly the wind chilled me to the core when I went out on deck with the kids. Thankfully, ferry rides were full of entertainment, and we could walk around the ship and change our point of view.

"Mom, look, it's a whale!" Rayna shouted out from the cafeteria. She sat facing the window and turned to kneel on the bench seat.

Out the starboard side, we saw a humpback whale surface and dive down again.

"How many times do they dive like that before they come all the way out?" she questioned.

"I think it's three. Keep your eye out to see him again," I answered.

We'd learned some of the patterns to note in the whales we saw from the staff on the ferry. Spotting whales was a common occurrence, but we were all enthralled with the new-to-us phenomenon.

"There he is again!" Rayna announced even louder. "That's two times now he's come up."

I moved from my seat to watch beside her. The dark ocean was smooth this morning, and we'd seen a few groups of whales earlier. "Wow, they sure are amazing, how they dive down like that. I wonder what they are eating for breakfast?"

"Ha, Mom, you're funny. They don't eat breakfast like us," she corrected me. "They're always snacking."

We watched in silence for the whale to resurface. Eagles flew over the large ferry. Exhausted from the long time on ship, I felt my eyelids sinking. We'd only rented two cramped berths, and attempting to share a bunk with Laura, I'd hardly slept the night before. Thank God we'd dock in Wrangell soon and be on our way to Bill's brother's place.

Rayna's squeal jolted me. "He's back and—Mom!" she shouted. "He's breaching!"

The whale launched itself into the air and came crashing down to the water's surface, creating a large splash. Rayna cheered and clapped.

"I can't wait to tell Grandma about the whale," she said before sitting back down at the table.

"She'll be impressed for sure," I answered as I looked around the cafeteria for Bill, who'd gone to find more eggs. He'd missed the show.

"How much longer, Mom?" Rayna questioned as she scraped her plate clean.

"I think the captain announced our arrival for Wrangell in a couple of hours. We might want to move to the front deck so we can watch for land soon. Remember the closer we get to land, the more animals we might see."

"Yeah, that sounds fun."

I appreciated Rayna's excitement. Our older kids were not as thrilled and moved about the ship between decks, watched a couple of movies in the small theatre, and played card games in the cafeteria. Thankfully, meandering from spot to spot was an option, unlike traveling in a vehicle.

"What did the captain say that island is?" Rayna asked, pointing out the window to the wooded land next to us.

"It's Etolin, and that it's known for its elk hunting. Although, I can't imagine what it would be like hunting in a thick forest like that."

Back in Oregon there were plenty of wooded areas, but the timber wasn't tangled on a steep, rocky surface like what I saw on Etolin.

Bill set his plate on the table and pulled out his chair next to me. "Sounds like I missed some excitement. Here, I brought you more coffee." Bill set a paper cup filled with black coffee on the table, and the steam rose in the air.

"Thanks." I smiled at him and blinked, trying to moisten my dry eyes.

"Daddy, how big is our boat gonna be?" Rayna inquired, sipping her orange juice.

Bill used his fork to break the yolk of his eggs and sprinkled his plate with pepper from the shaker. "About eighty feet."

"This big?" Rayna held her hands out wide.

Bill and I laughed. *Thank God, no.* But in my mind the boat wouldn't ever be big enough to give us the space we needed from each other. I loved my family, but I was rejuvenated by the alone time I got every day.

"It's like this, think of how big our house is and make it twice that size."

"Daddy?"

Chapter 3

Bill's mouth was full of toast, and here came the onslaught of five-year-old questions.

Bill finished chewing and took a sip of his coffee. "Yes?"

"Will I help you fish? Will I be big enough to help?"

Bill smiled. "There will be work for everyone. Trust me, you're big enough to help on our boat."

I watched Bill eat his hearty food and Rayna as she eyed her Daddy. She adored him and took in Bill's mannerisms and speech. It was a delicate balance beam with children watching our every move and our knowing that the impressions we gave them would last a lifetime. I saw myself in Rayna. How she watched people intently and picked up on the slightest change. I teetered with obsessing over details because I didn't just notice them, they blared at me. However, Bill assured me the positive aspect of my attentiveness was that I was alerted to danger and suspicion and that it could be used for good.

The ferry gently swayed, and I felt the movement propel us in a slight turn to the right. The boat rounded near the island's edge, and the waters opened up before us. Overhead, an announcement began. "Folks, we're nearing the last leg of our trip into Wrangell. We are continuing in the Stikine Strait with Woronkofski Island on our right and Zarembo on our left. Soon we will enter Sumner Strait, where we often encounter high winds off the Stikine River. No need to worry, waters are calm today. Enjoy the rest of your trip, and we'll make another announcement when we're thirty minutes from docking."

"I'll go find the kids," I said, then left the table to wander the ferry searching for the rest of our crew.

In my mind, I went over the day set before us. Driven to precisely plan major events, I'd asked Bill pointed questions about our trip and the obscurity of his answers gnawed at me. He wasn't bothered by the unknowns of where our fishing vessel was docked or how we'd prepare the boat in time for the first opener. Perhaps it was my lack of trust in others that propelled me to have my own plan in place.

As I walked out the door of the ferry and onto the outer deck, the cool air blasted my face, a stark reminder of the drastic changes ahead of us. Although they were temporary, they still threatened to teeter me like the swaying of the ship on the waters. Subtle yet present. My kids were huddled under an awning at the stern of the boat. The covered area was for summer travelers to tent under. Apparently, it was also an area for playing jump rope and tag. I paused to watch my children duck and spin in their games. I waved and walked past their cheery presences to the railing. The water behind the large ferry created a gigantic wake and the ripples spread wide behind us. A beautiful pink tinge hung on the tips of the clouds from the sunrise. God's presence was in His Alaskan creation. I couldn't deny it. Nor could I deny the uneasy sense of chaos about to explode within me when we docked. I closed my eyes and felt the misty air sprinkling my cheeks. Concentrating on my breathing, I inhaled and paused to pray the prayer that rose from within me.

Help me, God, to be strong today. I need to be steady and positive for the sake of my kids.

"Mom?" one of the girls called out, and I turned to face her. "Want to play a quick game of double-Dutch before we dock?"

I blinked back the tear that'd surfaced and walked toward her, pushing a smile across my lips. "Sure," I answered, hoping I'd masked the uncertainty the day represented.

CHAPTER 4

WE DROVE OFF THE FERRY RAMP ONTO A DARK, PAVED road at the edge of the island. The exhaust from the vehicle in front of us hung in the cool air. The road from the ferry terminal wound past well-kept houses on the main street. A tinge of wood smoke tickled my nose. Clean sidewalks lined the roads of the quiet island. With each moment, I aimed to take in the scene of the quaint city and make note of our new surroundings.

"Steve said the harbor is around five miles out of town." Bill casually held the steering wheel with his left hand and looked from side to side, presumably taking in the new sites.

The road meandered through town, and we passed a couple of churches mixed among the houses, a clinic, and a Quick Stop with a gas station. The main part of town was behind us as we passed the cemetery on both sides of the road and drove close to the water's edge. The rocky beach glistened in the low light, and the gray ocean waters lapped the shore. Birds flew down close to the water and landed on the small beach to the right.

"I see a harbor. There, Dad, is that it?" Daniel queried as the two-lane, paved road neared a protected harbor with numerous boats.

"Nope, that's not the one we're headed for. Do you recognize any of the kinds of boats we talked about?" Bill asked, pointing to the rows of boats tucked in close. While on the long ferry ride, he'd taught the kids about fishing vessels and quizzed them on their uses: sanning, gill netting, crabbing, and sport fishing. He was a patient teacher, and I adored how he dived in, wanting to include each of us. As he'd explained to me on our short walks out on the ferry deck, he noted the necessity of the whole family being educated about the new occupation. I'd not made the effort to memorize the terms and hoped our oldest son, Rob, was keen on learning the trade so he could be the most help to his dad.

We continued following the water's edge on our right with houses up on the rocky hillside to our left. The view must be astounding for the people who called the island home. "How far away do you think that island is?" I asked, pointing to the large tree-covered land mass across the water.

Bill tapped the steering wheel. "Probably a couple of miles."

"Look, it's a sea otter." Daniel called out from the back.

I searched the nearby waves at the shore and found the dark-colored otter he referred to. It bobbed in the wave, looking toward land as though it was curious why there were newcomers.

The kids chimed in about what had caught their awestruck attention. Laura declared it was the otter, and the other kids were excited to see their cousins. I gazed out at the deep ocean, attempting to fathom how we'd manage living in such a small space. There were many things to do to get ready for the family adventure, and the overwhelming tasks ahead formed a weight on my chest, pushing me back into my seat.

Bill stopped his rhythmic taps on the steering wheel and pointed ahead of us. "There it is. Shoemaker Harbor."

A rock wall surrounded the harbor for protection and pine trees nestled in close to the rocky parking lot we drove into. Across the lot, Steve climbed out of his truck, followed by three of his kids. They ran to us while we parked our truck and ambled out.

It'd been a couple of years since Steve had visited Oregon and since his subsequent introduction to his enthusiastic life in Alaska. Had this dream been brewing in Bill all along? Did he guard his ideas from me like the harbor's rock walls guarded it from the crashing waves of a stormy sea? Or perhaps I'd bypassed the clues leading up to our journey.

I knelt down to give my little nephew Neal a hug and stood to shake Steve's hand. The commotion of the moment whirled around me like a dirt devil off the paved road back home. The kids cheered, the men laughed, and my mind spun to grasp the weight of how far we'd come. A hand rested on my shoulder, and I looked to see Stanna, her gaze drawing me in.

"It's okay, Mom," she whispered.

God, help me snap back to the present.

Putting my arm around Stanna, I tugged at her for a side hug and smiled. The two of us lingered behind, following the rest of the family, who hurried down the ramp to the dock.

"It's a lot to take in. How are you doing?" I asked.

"I'm not happy about leaving my friends or missing out on my summer job at the pool." Stanna shrugged next to me.

"Honey, I didn't even hear you complain for one sec—"

Before I finished my sentence, I heard a scream, and we rushed down the ramp to see where it came from. Everyone was huddled in the middle of the walkway on the cement dock. "Mom," Rayna cried out. "We saw a sea lion."

Hurrying my steps, uncertain if a sea lion encounter was safe or not, I exclaimed, "Wow."

The group spoke with excited voices, and my racing heart settled in my chest.

Rayna narrowed the space between us and ran to me. "Mom, it was so cool. We heard a loud puff of air and then he came out of the water over by that boat." She inhaled deeply, then shrilled, "He was so close to us."

I searched Bill's eyes. I'd know from him whether to embrace the moment or not. Any animal with the name *lion* in it sounded dangerous to me. Finding Bill's eyebrows raised, I was uncertain of how to react.

Steve spoke up. "Stay together here in the middle. They're dangerous creatures, and they could knock you off the dock. Fortunately, we don't see that much of them down here. No need to be afraid; the loud noises we're making are scaring him, and he's moved on. I'm sure he was curious and looked up to see what was going on." After a minute, Steve motioned us to follow. "The boat you'll be on is here on the end." He turned and walked ahead of the group guiding us.

I shuffled over to Bill, put my arm around his waist and looked up at him. "That sounded scary," I whispered.

"Startling for sure," he answered back, and we walked toward the fishing vessel we'd found to rent for the season. "But...you and I, we've seen scarier."

That was an understatement, considering what had ignited the idea of being here. I still had nightmares of the panther lunging at Bill.

Bill pointed to a long wooden boat tied to the dock and bobbing in the water. I couldn't fathom cramming into the cab with everyone for days on end, nor the work it would take to be ready enough to untie the boat, wave goodbye, and launch out to the open water. We'd drawn up list upon list in anticipation of this new adventure.

The kids and I stood around and inspected the mussels attached to a tall pole that was part of the pier, while Bill and Steve talked about the boat from a distance. Later this afternoon, we'd meet the owner, tour the vessel, and go over details.

I inhaled the salty air and listened to the sound of seagulls overhead while I watched my kids as they explored the space on the dock and talked to their cousins, asking questions about the different boats they saw. This was a new world in sight, smell, and sound. It represented change, challenge, and obscurity. I felt like an onlooker watching it all happen and wondering how it would all turn out. Did I have the fortitude to embrace it? Maybe it was the exhaustion of traveling, but a surge of excitement rose to the surface while an ache in my core revealed I was well beyond my comfort zone.

THE KIDS RAN DOWN THE SET OF STAIRS TO THE beach ahead of Bill and me. From Shoemaker Harbor, we'd gone back to town to get some groceries, then we'd walked several blocks to explore a beach with the kids since the tide was going out. At the top of the stairs, the sign read, *Petroglyph Beach*. A cool breeze from the ocean nipped at my nose, and I reached in my pocket for a tissue.

Bill reached for my hand. "I can hardly believe we're here. I've imagined what it would be like, but this is way better."

"Oh, what is it that has you mesmerized?" I queried, curious about what had caught his attention.

"Everything." He gave my hand a squeeze.

We continued down the stairs and the kids stood waiting at the bottom.

"Uncle Steve said there's petroglyphs down here and you'll find them etched in the rocks when you scour. Go ahead and pair up and see how many you can find, but don't go beyond that large rock." Bill pointed to a distinct part of the beach where a rock divided the space.

"What is that? A petrogly—" Rayna stalled out in her question.

Bill laughed. "It's a carving in the rocks. Here"—Bill reached for her hand—"I'll search with you, then you can look more with Laura."

Stanna stood up from where she was squatting nearby. "Here." She handed me a piece of sea glass. "It's your favorite color."

The smooth aqua glass was cool in my hand, and I admired it before placing it in my pocket. "Thanks." I smiled at her.

With her gentle manner, her willingness to pitch in and help, and her generosity with compliments, she'd mirrored me in many ways over the years. I appreciated her courteous ways and their rippling effect in her grateful and hopeful outlook. She was becoming a young woman whose character shone like the glistening sea glass.

"I found one," Rob called out about twenty feet ahead of us. He squatted down and ran his fingers along the surface of a large rock.

We all hurried to examine it. I couldn't picture what kind of designs we might find on the rocks. Rob rubbed his hand over the carving of an image similar to a whale.

"Wow, that's neat," I said as I leaned over next to him. "How long do you think it would take to do that?"

"I don't know," Daniel said.

Rob answered, "A sign at the bottom of the stairs said no one knows who made all these carvings. The people who are native to this area don't claim to have made them. Maybe someone was shipwrecked here." He pretended to jostle a sword. "Aye, maybe it was pirates."

We laughed at Rob's silliness, then we continued searching —more diligently now that he'd spotted a carving. It was like hunting for a buried treasure. The kids scattered, watching the ground and scurrying from one large rock to another. Soon, they were calling out their discoveries one by one—swirls that looked like shells and images like faces and birds.

Perhaps I'd fixated too much on my own resolve instead of the treasures we might find along the way, like the petroglyphs nestled in the rocks on the beach. I'd taught my kids not to be nearsighted, to look beyond what was directly in front of their faces, and here I was, doing the opposite.

I looked around with a new lens and saw my energized family as they scoured the beach and spoke with excited voices when they picked up treasures from among the rocks.

Bill called out, "A few more minutes and we'll need to head out to Uncle Steve's so your mom and I can go look at the boat."

We'd designated a time to meet with the owner and sign paperwork for the lease. I didn't think I'd have any thoughts to share since this was beyond the scope of any kind of agreement I'd ever been involved in. Leasing a boat and living and working on a fishing vessel was as familiar to me as borrowing a submarine and plunging down to the ocean bed. I was certain, though, that I wanted to see the boat alone with Bill and not with the kids asking numerous questions while we tried to focus on the details. Thankfully, Steve and his wife Kim had agreed to let the kids visit at their house, where we'd be staying until the fishing season began.

The kids' pockets bulged with sea glass, shells, and polished rocks as they bounded up the stairs to the road. All the way back out to the main part of town, they talked about their discoveries and conjured up stories of how the petroglyphs had been made on the tip of Wrangell Island.

We piled into the truck and traveled the same main road through town and out to Steve and Kim's place. I blinked when I saw the tiny house at the top of a small hill. It didn't look big enough for Steve's family, never mind the seven of us. "How far is the harbor from here?" I asked, noting that we'd passed it more than a few miles ago.

"I think..." Bill stalled. "It's about six miles." He tapped the steering wheel and turned on the windshield wipers as a light rain began to fall.

"That's a decent distance to go back and forth. Not like we can just walk there," I stated, giving my comments freely. I'd assumed we'd skip over to the dock from Steve's, carrying our things and take our time setting up the boat as comfy as possible.

Bill gave me a questioning look. "Yes, it is. We'll have to drive."

I shook my head. "I'd pictured it differently."

"O-kay." Bill drew out a response. "Don't worry about things ahead of time. We'll figure it out."

"I know we will, but if we can streamline efforts, it'll be less hassle for sure. Juggling the kids at someone else's home and trying to help you all at once seems daunting."

"You're an expert at that. You keep all of us reined in back home. I'm sure you'll be fine. It won't be that long before we're all on the boat watching the sunset together," Bill assured me.

I'd felt like a failure in times past when I'd planned out how we'd tackle a project, made sacrifices to be productive, and then something interfered, toppling our efforts and dragging them out. It was so much work to gain momentum and pull it back together. I preferred working with concrete goals and choosing the best and most direct course of action, then following through with it.

The suburban jostled on the rocky driveway to Steve's house. Our kids asked numerous questions, and their voices buzzed around my head like a swarm of bees.

I reminded myself that I wasn't a new mom swimming in an ocean of uncertainty. As experienced parents, Bill and I were raising our children to walk with the Lord, and this was one more step in that direction.

Take baby steps. I reminded myself. *One little inch at a time and it will come together. Channel the determination, and don't let fear of the unknown swallow you.* Yes, a channel would be a good image to remember in the future.

As I opened my door, a verse from Proverbs Three came to mind that I'd memorized years ago. "Trust in the Lord with all thine heart and lean not unto thine own understanding. In all thy ways acknowledge Him, and He shall direct thy paths."

I let the verse form a prayer, and I prayed to God as I walked up the steps.

Alright, Lord, guide my determination so that I'm walking with You.

CHAPTER 5

That evening, at the kitchen table, the adults studied nautical charts and discussed the geography of the general area. A working knowledge of the islands, currents, and tides was like a whole area of expertise all on its own. Perhaps later, I could look the charts over more carefully so I could orientate myself. I loved looking at the map when we drove, and I assumed it'd be similar when we fished. Bill would drive the boat, and I'd help navigate.

"And this is a fish finder," Steve stated as he handed Bill a black contraption with wires hanging out of the back. "You should have one in your boat already. It not only helps with fishing, but with seeing the terrain of the land beneath you. It uses sonar to communicate the fathoms below."

I had a new respect for Steve, for all that he'd learned during his time in Alaska, and now he was willing to pass it on to us for our short season in Wrangell area.

The kids' loud voices echoed in the small house. Even though the noise pierced my ears, I was delighted they had time to play. Soon enough we'd be packed into a bobbing boat, floating in the unfamiliar Pacific Ocean.

"I think you'll do well." Steve pointed to the kids playing

chase. "Your kids are old enough to take on a good part of the work." He looked across the table at me. "And hat's off to you. There's no way Kim would live on the boat with me. She's more than happy to keep the home fires burning while I'm at sea."

Staying back while Bill fished wasn't an option. For our family, it was all of us or none of us. Hopefully, after he tried his hand at fishing, the adventure would end and we'd be back stoking our woodstove, having bonfires out back, and eating s'mores with friends.

I shrugged off Steve's comment and smiled at Bill. "It looks like you've some great pointers. I think once we familiarize ourselves with the equipment on the boat, today, we'll have more questions."

I searched Bill's eyes, which danced with excitement. He raised his eyebrows at me, and his look of childlike anticipation reminded me of the time he told me of the road bike he'd borrowed to take me for a drive one evening when the kids were little. We'd reminisced of days gone by as we rode the country back roads for hours.

In his element, Bill went over more details with Steve, and he beamed as he spoke. I assumed Bill took on this portion of the adventure with a healthy pride. He was determined to work with integrity and excellence, and I appreciated this quality in him.

Bill looked down at his watch and then tapped the table. "We'd better get going to Shoemaker so we can meet Tom."

I nodded and Bill rose from the table. He whistled his call for our kids to freeze. When they all stopped to listen, he gave instructions for when we were gone.

We made our way to the harbor, taking in the sights of the huge forest we drove through, which ran alongside the ocean.

"This reminds me of northern California, with the huge trees near Santa Clara." I gave a short laugh. "On a smaller scale, but still big."

"Steve said he knows a couple who harvested trees here on the island, milled the logs, and built their home. Sound familiar?" He glanced over at me, quirked his eyebrow and looked back at the road.

A small deer scurried from the edge of the road up the hill to the right of us. Steve let go of the steering wheel and rubbed his hands together. "Hey, a little buck. I'll have to tell Rob. He was asking what kind of animals lived on Wrangell. I wasn't sure since it isn't part of the mainland."

"You're sure amped up about the boat. Look at you," I stated. "You're practically on the edge of your seat, cramped toward the front." I shook my head and curled a half smile.

Bill laughed aloud and shuffled back in his seat.

A fluttery feeling rose in my chest, and I reminded myself of my strategy for viewing the inside of the boat for the first time. Over and over, I replayed my anticipated response. I'd find positive things to tell my mom, like the safety features or a neat piece of equipment that'd make the job easier. Determined to make a mental list, I opened and closed my fist, reminding myself that I'd find five things: one for each finger.

"Thanks again for going along." Bill paused and reached for my hand. "For being my soulmate. I couldn't do this without you."

"Aw," I replied back. "I'm hoping for the best." My half-truth stung my throat. I held back all the reservations I'd tucked in and pushed my tenacious spirit forward with mixed emotions. I was hoping for the best for my own interests. Not his. Maybe with time I'd warm up and enjoy this dream of his with more passion, but in the meantime, I loved watching his excitement build.

We turned into the parking lot and a large man stood next to the ramp leading to the dock.

We stepped out of the truck and approached the stranger with smiles. Bill reached out his hand. "You must be Tom."

Chapter 5

"I am, it's Bill, right?"

"Yes," Bill replied, and they shook hands.

"This is my wife, Grace." I waved as Bill introduced me.

"Nice to meet you," I said as I looked into Tom's gray eyes. He didn't smile, and I wondered if there was truth in my statement about meeting him being *nice*.

He nodded in return and walked ahead of us. He spoke over his shoulder, and I strained to hear him.

"What's that?" Bill questioned as we hurried our steps to keep up.

"Where ya from?" Tom asked again as he stopped in front of the slip where the boat was tied off.

"Oregon, and you?" Bill asked as he put his hands in his front pockets.

"Juneau." Tom stepped up into the boat at the bow and moved a stool over for us to step onto.

Bill helped me up into the boat, and I stood on the slippery deck, looking for my five positive things. I noted that the boat could use a wash. Leaves were tucked in the corners, and moss was nestled beside totes that lay face down. *Does he use this boat? It looked unkept.*

Tom fumbled with keys for the door, and I couldn't understand what he said in his hushed voice.

I pushed back the thought of offering to pick the lock for him. It was a quirky skill I'd mastered over the years that wasn't always socially acceptable, but it sure came in handy for a quick entrance or escape.

Bill asked him about his fishing experience, and Tom glanced at him as he tried another key in the lock. "I worked alongside another vessel, and we fished a season or two, but I'm headed back north to familiar waters." He tried yet another key and the door opened.

I pulled my hood off my head and followed Bill into the cabin. As I walked through the doorway, I inhaled a musty smell. Instantly, I was transported back in time to a camping trip with my youth group.

I braced myself on the door as I closed it behind me, then froze as I looked out the small window carved into the door. The rain started to pour, pounding on the rooftop.

I closed my eyes and inhaled again, the smell only reinforced the ache triggered by the memory of that day. The musty sleeping bag was what I'd lain in as I watched the youth leader creep into the tent. He shouldn't have been there. He shouldn't have been asking us girls questions, and we should have pushed him out the moment we noticed him.

"Grace?" Bill called.

I blinked and turned to face him, trying to widen my eyes and bring myself to the present. "Yeah?" I questioned.

"C'mon over here, he has a couple of things to show us on the dashboard."

"You're lying. You're wrong. You must not have seen it right."

My mom's response replayed in my mind. It left me frozen, my feet planted in place, immovable. She didn't believe me. Why did she believe the best in someone else and not me? Wasn't I worthy of her trust? What had I done wrong?

"Grace," Bill said, and I heard the frustration in his voice.

Turning my head from side to side, I saw the inside of the boat but couldn't focus on what was before me. A miniature table, foggy windows—

Bill moved to me, took my elbow, and placed his hand around my shoulder. He leaned over and whispered, "I'm not sure what's going on, but can you help me here?"

A burn in my stomach rose to my throat, and I bit at my lip. Rubbing my hands on my legs, I squeezed my eyes shut and willed myself to look at Bill's face. Could he bring me back to the present? I let myself lean into his strong chest and followed his lead over to the driver's seat and the main controls of the boat. Tom pointed to some knobs and a radio, but I didn't hear

Chapter 5

him speak. His muffled voice was drowned out by my own thoughts.

The emotions of that youth group event were rooted in my core, and I couldn't let them go. Not one girl was hurt, but we had all been shocked at the thought that something awful could've happened. The idea of a leader misusing their position to sneak in our tent left me nauseated.

When I'd told my mom, her response had stunned me. "Did you see it *correctly?*" she'd questioned me and the girls.

I'd come away from that moment telling myself I'd always be observant, have excellent recall, and be mindful of body language and expressions. The experience would leave me an expert on sizing up a person or place, and I'd take safety and precautions seriously. Except, for now, I was failing, letting my emotions grip me and pull me down.

"Thanks, Tom. We'll talk some more and get back with you," Bill stated. He let go of my shoulder and held my hand as we walked out of the boat and stepped onto the dock and toward the ramp. When we reached the top, Bill spun on his heels. "Where are you? The whole time we were there, I could have sworn you were in another world." He momentarily dropped his hands to his sides and then crossed his arms. "Did you see anything he showed us?"

I strained a smile and held my stomach as I stammered out the only response I could muster. "I don't feel well." My white lie was laced with a ribbon of truth; I was sick from holding the weight of worry.

Bill searched my face with kind eyes. Did he believe me?

"What else is wrong?"

I couldn't keep my feelings from him any longer. "It's too different. The smell reminded me that I'm vulnerable because I don't know what we're doing. I wanted to see all the good things about the boat, but I couldn't. I only thought of how I've missed things before, seen them wrong?" I paused and looked at my feet. "I'm sorry."

Bill took me in his arms and gave me a gentle squeeze. "Remember, we're in this together with God. You've got to trust He'll help you when these waves of doubt threaten you. C'mon, let's go back to the kids. I'll tell you what I heard Tom say, and tonight…we'll pray."

I let Bill guide me to the truck. Perhaps he felt the hesitation in my body that continued to pull me back in time even though he needed me to help direct us forward.

INSTEAD OF TURNING RIGHT OUT OF THE HARBOR parking lot, we took a left following the road to town. Silence was an uninvited passenger tucked between Bill and me. The clouds hung low, obscuring our view of the other nearby islands, and the fog pressed in around us. We'd left the blue skies of Oregon for the gray days of marine life. I assumed many more overcast days were to come.

"I tell you what, how about instead of going back to the kids, I take you on a short drive? We can make some mental lists before we're greeted with a million questions."

Bill was offering a reprieve. I sank back into my seat, appreciative of the breathing room. "Sounds good. What was your impression of the boat? It appeared unkept with all that moss on the deck." I scrunched my nose.

"This is a rainforest; there's going to be moss growing on everything. I'd admit, it's a bit rougher than I'd hoped for, but we're not buying it, just signing a short-term lease. If you're concerned about the mechanics of the motor, we could have a boat inspector do a pre-buy to rule out anything major."

Bill offered convincing reasons to move forward as he turned the vehicle onto a different road. We approached the local school and a ball field.

I twisted a loose strand of hair hanging at my shoulders as I attempted to recall anything noteworthy about the boat, but I couldn't bring anything to mind. *God, help me to see what needs to be revealed, good or bad.* Would He make it obvious?

"I'm weighing the decision heavily on the recommendation of Steve. He said Tom is an experienced fisherman looking to get back to his home north of here in Juneau. I can relate to his need for change. Perhaps he's been distracted by some pressing needs?" Bill questioned.

My compassionate man hoped for the best, whereas I was leery when luck and chance were big factors in the equation. "I suppose that might be the case. Other than the fact that it's musty inside and has a grimy deck, is it ready to go?" I was beginning to accept the fact that I wasn't able to conjure any images of how we'd fit on the boat or make it our temporary home. Nor could I remember how many beds I saw or where the bathroom was.

"Yup, it's ready," Bill stated.

We followed the road down a long sweeping hill and some buildings came into view to the right.

"Hey, it's the airport." Bill pointed toward the Wrangell Airport sign on the small building.

Seeing the airport reassured me that I wasn't as far from the civilization I was used to. The large jet parked on the tarmac looked like it was set to take off soon.

I cleared my throat and looked down at the seat for a water bottle. *There must be some water here somewhere.* I gulped back with a dry throat, knowing I would have to face my shortcomings of not finding my five points of interest.

"Babe, there's too much at stake to linger here. Remember we were going to hit the ground running tomorrow, get things ready? The tides don't wait. They'll swell whether we're out on the water or not." Bill looked straight ahead as he drove up the hill toward more houses.

"Alright, let's do this," I stated matter-of-factly, realizing I wasn't in a position to steer us away from what we'd set out to do. I'd have to muster up the courage to face the boat as it was and realize my short-term challenge would be worth the long-term gain. I would have to leave behind the teenager who'd run five miles after her mom doubted her and be the wife and mom who had more sense than to let a stinky boat drag her down.

CHAPTER 6

I ROLLED UP MY SLEEVES AND REACHED INTO THE cart we'd used to haul supplies from the truck to the dock. The kids formed an assembly line from the edge of the boat up into the cabin. The first shrimp opener started in less than forty-eight hours, and the many tasks ahead felt like a tsunami threatening to wash me out to sea. The goal we'd set for ourselves was to launch from the harbor, familiarize ourselves with the first location, and wake up ready to process shrimp as a tender; a vessel for commercial ishing boats to offload their catch. I'd overheard Bill and Steve discussing how long it would take to travel by boat and arrive in time, and I thought he'd said a day. Surely it couldn't take that long.

"Wow, Mom, this is a lot of food," Stanna stated as she reached for the case of peaches and took them from me.

"I wasn't sure how much to get for seven people," I answered as I gathered an armload of boxed crackers and placed them in her hands. The amount of bulk food I'd purchased at the local City Market grocery store in the center of town was convenient. However, when I saw the price of what I'd piled into two carts, my eyes bulged. The cashier's mouth curved a closed smile. I was certain they'd seen it before—a newcomer plunging into commercial fishing.

Stanna lifted a couple of bags out of the cart and handed them to Rob. He'd been assigned to go over the edge of the boat with the supplies and hand them to the middle kids who'd scurry them to the cabin.

"The food looks great, Mom," Stanna added. "Thanks for asking me to help plan some meals. Although, I'm certain we won't grow weary of PBJ's. I know I can't seem to get enough of them."

I flashed her a quick smile and tensed as I worked to conceal my surfacing emotions as we prepared for life in the musty fishing vessel. The busyness of the morning and delegating tasks distracted me from my racing heart and the pricking sensation running up and down my arms. I needed strength to face the day.

I heard Bill call out to the kids as they finished loading up our household items. Narrowing my eyes, I moved methodically to check off the items from the lists Bill and I had made.

A voice called out from across the boat slip. "Hey, don't forget"—

I looked over to where a man stood on the deck of his aluminum vessel and waved at us.

—"you know what they say, red sky at morn, sailors take warn." He pointed upward.

Bill shouted back, "Thanks for the word, but we've got to make it there tonight."

Unsure if they'd met before, I watched Bill's face for a sign of recognition as he nodded and went back to his task of securing a buoy on the side of the boat.

I turned, noting the spruce-filled hillside behind me and the scarlet sky shining a contrasting glow on the treetops. Was it wise to venture out in spite of the old adage that a morning sky painted red signaled a change in weather? I scanned the dock. All our items were safely loaded. It was time to step onboard.

"C'mon up, my amazing Grace." Bill called down to me. His wide smile spread across his face, and I noted the compassion in his eyes. He knew the apprehension this day represented for me. This morning before we got out of bed, we'd prayed together, asking for God's peace.

After climbing on board, I smoothed my pants with my hands and placed my hands on my hips. This was coming together. Our family was working as a team.

"Kids, come here." Bill strode close to me and put his arm around my waist. "Let's hold hands and pray before we set out."

We formed a circle, and I held onto Bill and Stanna's hands.

"Dear Lord, we thank You for this day and all it means to us as a family. Please go before us and be our strong and mighty tower. Be our lighthouse, God, and show us the way. Also, we ask that You bless our time. In Jesus name we pray, Amen." Bill's prayer finished, and he gave my hand a squeeze.

I released the hands I held as well as the clench in my jaw that I'd had for most of the morning. Pasting on a smile, I brushed at my coat sleeves, walked over to the edge of the boat, and looked down into the sea. The gray waters were calm and lapped at the boats in the harbor and dock.

I inhaled the fresh salty air and paused. *God, You know my heart, my fears, and the day ahead. I need You.*

Stepping aside from usual morning routine, I didn't linger over coffee or go for a walk. I'd known I would need to guard my heart and push on as my senses escalated in anticipation of this moment.

I hated the fact that I was triggered by the musty smell. The overwhelming aroma was common here in the Tongass National Forest. I wasn't going to escape it.

Daniel and Rayna called out, "Mom, we've got a surprise for you."

Forcing a smile, I cocked my head to the side and hesitated, but they waved me over. I walked through the doorway and into the cabin of the boat. The kids held their hands up to their chins, fists clenched in excitement. I sniffed and looked around. On the stove was a small pot, and steam rose from the top.

"It's your favorite: orange and cinnamon." Daniel said as he joined me by the stovetop and stirred the boiling mixture. In the fall and early winter, he'd watched me gather orange peels, cinnamon sticks, and cloves and boil them on the woodstove to add a sweet and woodsy smell to the house during the damp, rainy days.

"Ah, that's so sweet." A tear formed in my eye.

I gave him a hug and took in a deep breath. The scented water had masked the dank, funky smell that had stung my senses the other day.

"Love ya, Mom." Daniel spoke softly, returning my embrace. "Daddy said you'd like this, especially today."

I stood holding him and allowed the wave of comfort to ease my shoulders and bring me to a familiar place where I knew God would help me one step at a time.

AS BILL NAVIGATED THE BOAT, THE KIDS AND I skirted back and forth between spaces, organizing the supplies, food, and gear. I'd no clue there would be so many emergency-related items to affix in sight and within reach.

Bill hummed a familiar tune, and the kids sang along. I tried to be still and let relief set in. We'd launched successfully. We were on schedule. And the blast of musty odor was softened by my thoughtful family.

Thank You, Lord, for my family and where You've brought us.

Chapter 6

Gratitude for simple things was something my mom seemed to have mastered, and in this moment, I hoped it was a quality that I'd emulate and that my kids would, in turn, take on. A godly legacy was my dream, and perhaps this new adventure would provide ample opportunities for Bill and me to show our kids these important values.

Daniel and Rob stood out on the deck of the boat, close to the edge.

"You guys, back up," I raised my voice out of fear and rushed at them.

Their startled reaction suggested I'd overreacted.

"O-kay," Daniel answered reluctantly. He stepped back, while Rob lingered near the edge.

"Dad said it was okay to be close, just no fooling around," Rob answered, motioning toward the cabin. He stepped back with a sly grin, as though he was amused by something else and began to walk away.

"Rob, you need to acknowledge me," I stated matter-of-factly, needing to address his subtle defiance.

"Hmm?" He turned his head and looked past me, making a point that'd he set his mind on something else.

"Do you think you and Daniel can find something to do where you are in the center of the deck and not near the edge?"

"Yup," he answered as he sauntered over to some rope that lay in a bundle.

"Grace, come here a minute," Bill called out.

Trying to live up to my Grace-ful name, I tiptoed across the slick deck over to the cabin and poked my head in. "Yes?"

"Come here. I want to show you a few things." Bill pulled out a chart and set it on a table near the helm. "This is Wrangell." He pointed to the island tucked near the mainland. "And this is where we're headed. We'll go along Sumner Strait out to the open water, then head south and skirt over to POW."

"POW?" I searched Bill's face, unsure of the acronym.

"Sorry, it's short for Prince of Wales. It's this island, here." He tapped the spot on the chart. "We're set to anchor there as the tender." He pointed to a cove near the dot on the map labeled Craig.

"Craig?" What made you choose this spot?"

"It's the largest town on the island, and it's the main point of commerce. Namely, it's where the buyers are for the shrimp we'll process."

I scanned the chart, and it all appeared overwhelming. So many names scattered the plot. How could one make sense of it all in a short span of time? With each moment like this, I appreciated Bill's sense of direction and the fact that he'd worked hard to become comfortable coasting to our next adventure. If something were to happen to him, we'd probably drift into the open ocean and never be recovered because I wouldn't know where to begin. The thought chilled me.

"You okay?" He tilted his head.

"Yes, there's so much here. How'd you pinpoint this exact job and line this all out? I know I haven't been your tagalong for this one."

"Things have fallen into place, but I've also spent a lot of time researching and taking wise counsel." Bill pulled me in for a side hug, then went back to what I called the steering wheel and manipulated some of the controls. "There, we're on autopilot." He took a step back and crossed his arms, appearing satisfied.

I moved toward him. "You're not going to leave it like that." My words came out more as a statement than a question.

Bill chuckled. "I was only testing it. I won't leave it. Not yet anyways."

I turned from him and raised my eyebrows. I didn't know why he thought I could come alongside him in this. My mother-hen instincts were fully engaged when we first stepped onto the ramp, down the dock, and to the door to search for and count the kids, making note of where they all were. Bill and I had always been adventurous, even teetered on the edge of danger as we worked with the wild animals on set. But this was uncharted territory—bringing my babies into the equation.

"Get everyone together to put everything in its place. If we hit rough waters, we don't want things crashing down on us. Plus, it'll be good to get the kitchen set up and the bedding situated. Once we're near Craig, it will be all hands-on-deck for business, not setting up house." He moved back to his post at the controls.

His to-do list was a welcome distraction. I no longer had to focus on the sense that I was a half-knit sweater with the yarn pulling from side to side and unraveling my peaceful emotions. The usual mom-tasks and boat duties were an unfamiliar mix with a constant reminder of potential danger out in the water. I hoped that with everyone in one place, everything unpacked, and some food in the small oven, we could kick back, play some games, and pretend we were back home gathered for a peaceful evening after a day's work.

CHAPTER 7

Bill, Rob, and Daniel sat at the controls of the boat while I lingered at the table with the girls and my coffee. The boat's gentle rocking reminded me of the soothing sway of the porch swing, and sitting with my mom in the cool of the day. If this first peaceful evening on the boat was a foretelling, I was sold on the idea of a temporary assignment at the sea.

Stanna prepared supper for us, and the aroma of the savory steaks hung in the air, pushing out any reminder of the dank dungeon I'd first imagined the boat to be.

Laura, my quiet and reserved daughter, wandered from the table over to where the guys were situated and listened in. She was my observant ten-year-old, slowly coming to the age of a young woman. I'd noted the tears that welled in her eyes at times of frustration, but she held them back. It was rough being ten. The childish tendencies fought to survive, while the yearning to attach to the older crew pulled her as well. The pendulum was swaying, and she was holding on. I'd have to remember to hug her more and remind her it was okay to still be young and good to want to grow up, too. Would it make sense?

Rayna jumped up from the table and wiped her mouth on her sleeve. "Thanks again for supper. May I be accused?"

"It's *excused*, remember? Not accused." Her little mix-up was comical, and I chuckled.

"Babe? Is there any coffee left?" Bill moved over to the table with his mug.

"I emptied the pot, but I'll make you more. Have an all-nighter planned?" I knew the answer to my question, and I was glad it was him and not me. Watching out over the dark of the ocean for hours on end sounded like a good recipe for boredom.

As I filled up the carafe with water, I noted a faint shrill from the wind outside.

"Yeah, an all-nighter for sure," Bill said. "But I'll need you to be up a couple of times to check on me to make sure I'm awake or relieve me for a few minutes so I can make my rounds."

"Oh, golly," I blurted without thinking.

The wind on the water and boat grew louder, and I turned my head toward the ocean.

Bill placed his hand on my arm. "Don't worry. With time, Rob will be able to help with the night watches and checking the anchor. We'll find a rhythm that involves some teamwork. I've got the best crew there is."

I smiled at his compliment. "Alright." I shuffled my feet.

The wind's howl built up around us and I turned to look at Bill. He rushed at the controls and gripped the wheel. "Move to your seats," he shouted to the kids, waving them back.

The noise increased, and without being told, I knew this was the storm we'd been warned about by the sailor back at the harbor. The bow rose, and the items on the table began to slide back, threatening to fall. Stanna spread herself onto the plates and grasped a glass to keep them from falling.

Rob and Laura took seats close together, while Daniel and Rayna grabbed onto one another near me. We huddled at the table, unsure of the best place to hunker down. After cresting the wave, the boat plummeted downward and water sprayed the front window.

"It's a wind out of the south, blowing through the channel," Bill shouted above the squeal of the wind. He widened his stance to brace himself.

Was it common for winds to rise out of nowhere like this? If he was somewhere else on the boat and I needed to take control, could I rein us in? What if one of the kids were outside? We'd thought the waters were calm. Someone could have wandered out, thinking everything was fine. The thought caught my breath.

"It doesn't look like this should last long. We're about to shield ourselves with another island. Hold on."

His assuring words did not calm the tightness in my shoulders nor the grip I had on Rayna. I wanted to run from the squall and nestle myself away from the danger like when our contentious bull was loose on the farm and I'd climbed to the barn loft as a kid. Daddy would wander in calling my name and gather me in his arms. As a girl, I was concerned about myself. Now, as the parent, the weight I carried was for my children. Bill's words alone were not enough to keep us safe.

Lord, help us.

The prayer for God to intervene should have risen to my lips and been said out loud, but I froze in place, waiting for the next heave of the bow to obey the command of the wave.

Rayna huddled in closer, and I pressed into her, hoping to assure her, although I wasn't assured myself.

My heart raced as the boat crashed down again, and I braced myself. As the boat leveled, the angle we'd risen to flattening, I let out a sigh, knowing this was the signal. The waves were gone.

Was this a small taste of the storm brewing, like the warning from the sailor we'd heard on the dock earlier? Had we skirted the danger? My shoulders fell as I released the deep breath I was holding.

"That was unexpected," Bill said while holding the controls. He looked over his shoulder, searching my face. "You all okay?"

"Wow, Dad," Rob spoke up. "How'd you learn to keep calm and ride the waves?" He stood up as he talked, bending his knees and stretching out his arms as though he were on a surfboard.

The kids continued to ask Bill about the ocean, and I picked up the dishes off the table, determined not to ask questions. I assured myself that I could pick up clutter, wash pots and pans, make a grocery list, and help look at nautical charts, but I wasn't going to quiz Bill about managing the boat. It might as well be a spaceship orbiting the earth, it was so far beyond anything I'd imagined.

As I gathered items that'd fallen on the floor, someone's watch beeped the hour, reminding me of the hourly chime of the grandfather clock in my mom's living room. The tick-tock of the family heirloom's swinging pendulum was a rhythmic melody that'd calmed me when I took the time to hear it. Now, I was the one swaying to a beat I didn't know. I'd gone from embracing the journey, to searching my past for a familiar place to steal away. Laura wasn't the only one finding her way.

BETWEEN THE NAPS AND NIGHT WATCHES, THE evenings and early mornings were uneventful. I was curious whether the kids would nervously toss and turn in their new beds, but they managed to drift off easily and sleep soundly. I stretched in bed and sat up to find the hoodie that I'd tucked near my pillow.

Time for my new morning routine.

The cool air stung my bare feet, and I felt for my boots, which my socks were tucked into. The humidity still clung to my clothes, and I knew coming from a dry climate to one where the moisture clung to every fiber was going to be an adjustment for me.

Everything is different, God. My heart flowed in prayer, as it usually did during my quiet and alone time at the start of each day, telling God what He already knew and knowing He still wanted to hear from me. *I don't want to be the wet blanket. I know I need to be strong and show my kids fortitude. Help me start this day with a fresh outlook and hold onto You as my anchor when it gets bumpy. Amen.*

A calm sense that I could believe everything was going to be okay washed over me. I stood up, pulled my hoodie on, and walked out of the sleeping berth to the main cabin. I smoothed my clothes and looked directly out the window as I neared it. The rising sun over the large mountain reminded me that my God, who created the universe, would see this through to the end. It was a truth I firmly believed in my mind, but did my actions show it?

"Morning, amazing Grace." Bill announced as he came from behind a large bin in the center of the kitchen.

"Hi, honey." I wrapped my arms around his waist and reached up to give him a kiss, savoring the cocoon of his embrace.

"We're set to arrive on time in about a half hour." He lifted my chin. "By the way, you're doing a great job, rolling with this aquatic escapade. Your smiles cheer me on."

I held his gaze, nodding at his compliment. "I'm here, like I pledged." A lighthearted sensation pulsated through me. "For better or worse, high or low water."

Bill chuckled. "Is that how it goes? It's been a while since we said our vows."

Chapter 7

I looked down at the tall rubber boots I'd traded for the light tennis shoes I normally wore, then back to his quizzical face. "I'm promising to be there beside you, but will you reaffirm to me this is going to be a successful venture?"

Bill took my hand and led me to the controls where he moved to hold onto the helm. "I guess that depends on how you measure it."

I nestled in close to him, taking in the warmth of his embrace and the safety I felt in his powerful arms. Our alone time would have to be in small snippets, like a snuggle in the morning, watching the sun come up over the ocean.

The welcoming aroma of coffee filled the space, and I turned to see the pot was almost done brewing. I moved to pull a mug off a hook and set it on the counter. "Honestly, I've narrowed my standard of success on this mission."

Bill turned to face me. "What?"

"Not in a bad way. I just want, more than anything, for all of us to be safe. Yesterday scared me, and that was only a short stint of rough water." I poured my cup full of black coffee and took a sip.

He turned to face the front window. "I hear ya, I agree. That's what's in the bin. More safety items to go over with the kids. Today we'll practice our survival suits again. Would you pour me a cup too?"

The radio blared, and Bill and I jumped. The call sign for our boat was beckoned. Bill picked up the handheld mic and answered.

I moved over to the table, listening in to the conversation. I narrowed my eyebrows as the harbormaster asked Bill accusatory questions. What could we be guilty of in our short time on the ocean, and in waters unfamiliar to any of us?

Bill repeated his first and last name and his voice tensed as he fixed his gaze out the window. Normally, Bill was a patient man, rarely speaking loudly or harshly. "No, sir. That's not us," he stated with his mouth close to the mic.

The harbormaster reiterated firmly that we'd not be allowed in his harbor because of overdue fees.

Bill's shoulders stiffened, and he rubbed the back of his neck. "I've never been to this city before. This is our maiden voyage."

I sensed his frustration and closed my eyes. *God, help us to know what to do.*

The harbor master's stern instructions did not relent. "Either you pay the outstanding fees associated with your vessel, or you're not welcome here. Those are the options."

Bill let out a heavy sigh and scrubbed a hand across his face as he clicked the mic in his left hand. "Although we didn't incur those fees, we'll pay them." He shook his head and lowered his voice. "We're scheduled as a shrimp tender."

Letting him sort the details, I went to the back to rouse the kids and get the day started with them. We could help Bill by being ready for whatever unfolded. Hopefully, they'd jump in and listen, and the day would prove successful for all of us.

CHAPTER 8

THE KIDS AND I TIMED OURSELVES GETTING ON OUR survival suits, making it a game, cheering each person on during their turn. My stomach cramped from all the laughing as we wiggled our way in and tripped over ourselves. As I struggled my feet into the Gumbi-style suit, I breathed a prayer, pleading with God that I'd never have to put it on in the event of a true emergency. The practice was hilarious and cumbersome, but Bill's brother, Steve, had shown us a trick or two on the mainland before he set out and soon we'd streamlined our efforts.

"Mom, look." Rob's sleeves hung loose, and he untucked his arms and flopped them. "I'm like a gummy worm." We all laughed at his comical way of continually lightening the mood.

"Time to put those away and head to your practiced post." Bill spoke with a commanding presence. "Babe? Can you come here for a minute?"

"Sure." I set my suit down on the deck and went inside, giving the kids a thumbs up as I passed them.

Bill shut the door as he spoke. "It sounds like Tom, the owner, made quite the name for himself in the short time he used the boat down here."

I placed my hand on my hip. "Not our fault." I'd blurted out those words I'd wanted to say years ago when I'd been on the teen retreat. There were people in authority who used their position for their own gain—and someone else's loss. Here we were again, victims to someone else's poor choices.

"It's become ours. We've inherited his reputation, his dues—"

He stopped midsentence as the kids handled the bin in the doorway.

"All we can do is make sure we follow the rules, and hopefully people will see we're not like that." I was hopeful we'd make the best of the situation. We were always keen on obeying the rules of the land; surely, we'd do the same on the sea.

"You're right, I shouldn't have let it grab me." He picked up his cup of coffee, took a sip and smiled down at me.

I was pleased that I'd managed to help reassure the fears brewing in his core, and quickly returned to the kitchen.

The kids situated the bin and helped themselves to breakfast items: bagels and fruit cups. Farm-fresh eggs and milk from the neighbors weren't an option on the open water. However, I was looking forward to some fresh salmon when the opportunity presented itself. I sat next to Daniel and put some cream cheese on my bagel.

A minute later, Bill joined us. "Alright team, I'm going to go over the plan for the next hour or so. I'm about to shut off the engine and listen in for specifics on where we'll drop anchor. As the tender, it means other vessels will bring their catch to us. We process the shrimp, then offload to refrigerated containers for the buyers to pick up. I can't answer a lot of questions right now. I need you all to be quick to obey and not argue with instructions. We don't have time to waste; this is our job. I'm learning right along with—" Bill was cut off by a call on the radio directed at us. He moved and answered.

"We didn't think you'd be back after last time." The mystery caller stated.

Chapter 8

"This is Bill. We are new to this vessel." Bill articulated his words firmly, and I hoped the conversation didn't take an unpleasant turn with the kids listening in.

The caller returned with a comment. "Nevertheless, we'll be watching you closely. Stay out of my way, and I'll stay out of yours."

Bill put down the radio, shrugged his shoulders and stepped over to us. "This is a good lesson for all of us. The owner of the boat doesn't have a good reputation, and now we're going to have to prove ourselves."

Rob stood up and put his paper plate in the garbage. "What do you mean?"

Bill grabbed the coffee pot and refilled his cup. "We're going to show integrity, son. Do the right thing at the right time for the right reason. We've nothing to hide. This is a lucrative business where the stakes are high, and we've a lot hinging on whether people trust us or not."

Rayna stood up, placed both hands on her hips, and strutted over to Bill. "They better not say anything bad about my Daddy, 'cause it isn't true."

Bill set his cup down on the counter and scooped Rayna up in his arms. "If they do, I'll let you at 'em. Watch out guys, she's a tough one." He tickled her, and she squealed. Setting her down, he moved his gaze across all our faces, watching us. "Finish up breakfast, and let's do this."

I raised my chin and gave Bill a crisp nod. There were some hurdles to conquer, but we were a team ready to forge on.

"Alaska State Troopers. Please respond." The message came through loud and clear on the radio.

Who were they speaking to? I stood up and looked outside the window and saw a tall blue and white boat coming toward us.

The kids mumbled about the word *trooper* as Bill darted for the mic. "This is the vessel "Bail Out."

"Yes, this is the Alaska State Troopers. Permission to board your vessel?"

Bill looked over his shoulder at me and raised his eyebrows. He fumbled with the mic and cleared his throat. "Permission granted. Uh, hum, ten-four?"

Rob chuckled, "really, Dad? Ten-four?" He laughed some more.

Bill snapped his fingers, signaling enough. "Grace? We need the pile of paperwork I gave you. Did you put it in a drawer?"

I blinked rapidly, trying to recall what paperwork he'd given me. Everything passed through my fingers, but I didn't attach a sense of value to it since it was all new. "I...I'll look," I stammered, giving a quick nod and moving to search.

Tucking my hair behind my ear, I dug through some binders Bill had placed back on his bed. He'd mentioned it wasn't where they'd be stored but he needed to finish sorting on a flat surface. Ugh, why wasn't this at his fingertips and at the hull? How was I supposed to know what the troopers would be asking for? I grabbed all the binders and balanced them in my arms. How about all or nothing?

The kids were all huddled around the table pretending not to notice the escalating tension. Rob shuffled some cards and whispered to the others.

"Need a hand, Mom?" Daniel asked.

"Sure," I answered and stopped to let him take a couple of the binders from the top of the pile.

I shuffled my feet across the floor, careful not to drop what remained in my arms. In the future, I needed to be studious when it came to filing. There needed to be a way to keep it close and dry. This could be a job I kept for myself. It'd be a way to watch the business closely, as well. Was it profitable? Or was it one risk after another, depleting our savings?

Daniel held the door for me, and I stepped out on the deck.

Chapter 8

A trooper turned from where he stood, and a slow smile formed on his face when he saw me approach.

"Whoa," he said, looking at the pile in my arms, his one-word response stinging my ears.

Did I fumble the meeting? "I, uh-haven't got these all sorted yet, and I—"

"Nice to meet you. Let's take these inside and have a quick look. I didn't mean for you to dig these all out." The trooper pointed back to the cabin. "I only need to see a few things. Looks like you probably have your bases covered."

Bill took the binders from me and Daniel, and we formed a line back inside.

Stretching out his hand, the trooper narrowed the gap. "I'm Paul. This is quite the crew you have with you here."

"I'm Grace." I shook his hand. "And yes, we have a lot of help." I glanced over my shoulder at the kids, who mostly gave the officer shy smiles.

"I just need to see your crew member licenses, the ADF and G vessel registration paperwork, and your fishing permit." Paul held his ball cap in his hand and waved at Rayna, who was inching closer to Bill.

"Are you taking my Daddy to jail?" Rayna hugged Bill's leg.

Paul squatted next to her. "No, ma'am. What's your name, little lady?"

"I'm Rayna. My daddy says we value intensity, so you don't have to give him a ticket," Rayna stated as she loosened her grip on Bill and stepped away from him.

My eyes bulged, *intensity*? What was she talking about?

"Ha, you mean, integrity, Rayna," Stanna called out.

We all laughed, and I shook my head. It never ceased to amaze me what the kids *thought* we said and the words we *actually* said.

"Sounds like you're pretty smart, Rayna," Paul said, reaching into his vest pocket and pulling out a small piece of paper.

"Would you like a trooper tattoo? It washes off, but it'll make you look even tougher than you already are."

"Yeah!" She jumped up and down then spun on her heels. "I told you, I am tougher than you," she said, pointing her finger at Rob.

"Well, there's one for each of you. Can you give them out?" Paul handed Rayna a few more tattoos.

Bill held open a binder and flipped a few of the plastic inserts he'd placed inside to protect the papers. "It looks like it's all here." He extended it out for Paul to see.

"Thanks." Paul took the binder and pulled out his notebook from his pants side pocket and cleared his throat. "Are you aware of the dealings of the owner of the boat?"

Bill nodded. "We've started to hear a few things since we arrived."

"I admit, I was surprised when I came on board and saw you. I was ready for a duel, thinking it was him. I wish you the best, considering you're going to have to sell yourself before you can move forward." He flipped the pages in the binder. "Everything's in order here." He shut the binder and handed it back to Bill, then flipped open his notebook. Kneeling close to Rayna, he held out his pen. "I'd better make sure I write in here that I met a crew member of integrity named Rayna."

Rayna pulled her shoulders back and raised her chin. "Um-hm. That's me."

"I'll be seeing you around." Paul walked to the door. "If you have a minute, Bill, I have a couple of suggestions for you." He nodded toward the deck, and Bill followed him out.

Was his statement about selling ourselves true? What exactly did it mean? Were we going to have to seek out buyers?

God, where are you in this? Does this mean we've made the wrong choice? I feel numb to Your presence when all we keep getting is bad news. There wasn't time to waste. We needed efficiency, not a setback.

CHAPTER 9

Pulling my blanket close around my face, I scrunched my nose to see out the window but couldn't decipher anything. The fog created condensation on the windows like back home when I canned vegetables all day. However, the thick oppression of this fog on the ocean reminded me more of the times when I was sick with a fever, couldn't think clearly, and wondered if I'd recover.

This morning, my breaths felt shallow, and I sensed the weight of the moisture in the air was also wreaking havoc with my motivation to get up and face the day. A week into the shrimp opener, and we'd not met our fifty-percent holding capacity.

Last night, as I tossed and turned on the bunk, I pictured our boat bobbing in the ocean and threatening to sink with the weight of the shrimp no one wanted to buy from us. Doubt taunted me, threatening that we'd lose more than we put into our fishing venture. Finally, I'd willed myself to pray and pleaded for God to help calm me so I could sleep between my night watches. I felt a twinge of guilt for praying for what I wanted, especially since it had been days without breathing a prayer.

Rayna started to grind her teeth and the noise sounded like nails on a chalkboard. I shuddered and climbed out of bed, grabbing my coat, which hung nearby, and wrapping it around myself.

Bill mumbled to himself at the table, his back turned to me, and I walked closer, hoping to give him a little bit of a fright. He was so fun to scare. Inching one slow movement at a time, I saw he sat with his eyes closed. *Perfect!* I reached my finger to touch his ear, and he jolted in place, tossing the paper in his hand.

"Gol-ly!" he responded and shook his head. "Here I am having a serious talk with God, and you scare the life out of me."

"Happy to help. Just trying to loosen the mood on this dank morning." I smiled and shivered. The humidity worked its way to my core, giving me the chills.

"I was going over these charts and found the cove where we can meet the Japanese buyers." Bill tapped the paper on the table in front of him with a pencil.

"The what?" I'd wondered how this all worked. Bill hadn't mentioned the next step yet. Yesterday, a few shrimp boats offloaded their catch, and the kids and I helped secure the hold, but it didn't amount to much.

"I heard there are international buyers. The ones I've lined up are Japanese, and they've agreed to provide the containers and electricity for refrigeration. It takes a load off us."

"Literally." I moved to the window and wiped the condensation off with my sleeve. "Ugh, I can't stand not being able to see anything."

Bill stood up, came over, and put his arm around me. "I'll tell you what you see." He turned me to face him. "You see your family working together, they're laughing and having a great time. A little cramped at times, but they're in this together."

I shook my head. "Nope, that's not what I see. I see a fog so thick I'm not sure I would notice my hand in front of my face, and I don't see buyers lined up. The one you mentioned is great, but we can't keep doing this. We're moving at a snail's pace. Every day it costs us money to be here, wherever that might be."

Obsessively cleaning, organizing, and revisiting the check lists were my daily tasks for days on end. The cycle proved to bring me the satisfaction of knowing I could control a small aspect of the business of a tender waiting for fishermen. However, at this point, I wasn't convinced I could hold the pattern much longer without seeing that it mattered and that we were gaining. I crossed my arms and turned away to face the cabin. I replayed the scene from last night over and over in my mind: the crisp image of shrimp in the hold and the echo below. We were wandering half-empty with hopes someone would believe that we weren't the sly owner of the boat.

I turned my head to catch Bill's reaction to my spewing feelings. He watched me, and his eyes softened. He pressed his lips together, holding back his own emotion.

I continued. "We've been betrayed by the owner. There doesn't seem to be a way around it. I can't see how we can keep hoping for a happy ending. Shouldn't we be tossing a coin to help us decide which of the ten fisherman we should let approach us with their catch?" A taut feeling gripped my midsection, and I wrapped my arms around my waist. "No, here we are, vulnerable in the fog of despair—if we're honest with ourselves." I wanted to take back my words the moment they left my lips. I didn't want to accuse Bill.

His eyes narrowed. "You see the glass half-empty, I see it half full. We're both being honest, no one is lying. And we were rooked. I agree." Bill sat back down at the table and sipped his coffee. "However, we have to make the best of what we have. Let's see this through, and when it's over, we'll go back home."

"Okay." I agreed, knowing in my heart that I'd only consented to the last part of what he'd said: *we would* leave.

More than anything, I wanted to press fast-forward and transplant myself into my front yard where I'd be standing on the solid ground—standing on the foundation of faith and family we'd built there. Maybe once we were back home, we could pick up where we'd left off and discover a vision for the future of our family.

After unloading the shrimp, we traversed the calm waters near Craig. *What an absolute waste of time*, I'd told myself as I'd watched the reddish-brown spot prawn slide into the refrigerated sea container. The Japanese buyers were all smiles at the promise of more of the delicate gem of the southeast waters of Alaska. However, I sensed we might not return to offload another remnant.

I pulled out a small skein of yarn I'd purchased at the Wrangell grocery store and tore the paper pattern off the middle of it. I tried reading the directions, but they read more like Greek. I set the yarn on my lap. Could I find something besides cleaning to occupy my boredom and distract me from the thoughts of failure that hung over my head?

Bill tinkered with some contraption near the stern of the boat and the kids scurried around the cabin. The noise and commotion were beginning to irritate my last nerve.

"In five minutes, I'd like all of you to go outside and find something to do," I stated, raising my voice.

A couple of "okay, Mom" statements came in return, but I didn't look up.

Smoothing the knitting pattern instructions on my lap, I looked closer at the picture on the front. A woman with graying hair held a colorful dishcloth. Her kind eyes reminded me of my mom. I could make this for her. The idea sparked my interest enough to learn the stitches and create the simple project. I pulled at the yarn to unravel it a bit.

The boys began bickering over a compass they were spinning on the table.

I looked up from my project. "Alright, out." I paused and pointed my finger at them. "Go outside. Now."

They don't get it. I was so sick of this lull and all this empty time. How could I busy them without being their source of entertainment?

Rob, Daniel, Laura and Rayna filed out the door. Stanna was already helping her dad.

Good land, I hope they stay out all morning. I gripped my knitting needles. Maybe I could cast on the first row and at least get an inch or two done before they tumbled back in, disrupting my thoughts.

I let my memories of the times I'd tried to start new hobbies when the kids were young unravel. The pursuit of something creative was inviting when all the days of dirty diapers, making baby food, and cooking a warm supper for the end of the day meshed together. We'd come a long way in our family life, yet there were unique challenges for each stage.

For myself, I needed something to call my own and a welling of pride at having completed something. Months of waiting to leave for Alaska and now the uncertainty of the fishery gnawed at me like a small fox gnawing at its paw for release from a trap. Perhaps knitting a small washcloth would be the morsel of success I needed to propel me forward.

A crashing noise jolted me, and I stood up to look at the kids. I didn't see what had made the noise, and they shrugged their shoulders at me. I sat back down, crisscrossed my legs on my chair, and reread the pattern again.

This is useless. Why do I try to do anything?

The grocery bag I'd pulled the yarn from contained a few

more skeins, and I reached to pull out a couple of them to inspect the patterns on their wrappers.

From the bow, a clanging and drawn-out screech drew my attention, and I dropped the yarn on the floor.

Those kids! I'm going to have to—

Out the window, I saw Rob swinging on the rigging out over the open water and kicking his legs to thrust himself toward the boats' edge. "Rob!" I called out, yanking the door open as he landed safely in the boat. "Get, inside." I yelled, glaring at each of them. "Go...go and sit back there with your dad."

Without a clue of what to say about the horror of their *fun*, I marched inside behind them, shooting an icy glare at Bill.

"I'm done," I said, then turned and marched back to my bed, leaving them to face the fury of their father. I didn't care what he thought or what anyone else thought of my absence. There wasn't an ounce of patience left in me to ponder what could have happened if Rob had fallen in or was caught in the mess of the rigging.

We had no business being on a fishing boat in Alaska, trying to force ourselves where we weren't welcome. Clearly, I didn't know how to occupy my or the kids' time on the waters of this Pacific Ocean. A storm of discontent was brewing to the depths of my core.

CHAPTER 10

BILL CROUCHED NEXT TO WHERE I LAY IN MY BUNK. He'd come over to me that afternoon, after he'd taken a considerable amount of time to lecture the kids and hand out discipline to those who'd disobeyed outright. I'd cut myself off from hearing any of the conversation, afraid I'd explode at any minute. Kids were going to be kids, and I got that, but I was on edge with worry that their childishness could cost them a high price. Would I be there to help avoid the danger?

"One more month, then we'll pull anchor and go back." Bill offered.

My eyes closed. I envisioned the anchor cresting the water's surface, clamoring into its spot in the chain locker, and the boat motor propelling us away, back to Wrangell. Yes, an image of leaving was one I could hold onto.

"Okay," I said with my eyes closed. "I think I'll try and nap for a bit."

Without seeing Bill's face, I knew he looked at me with disappointment. He included me in everything he did, and I was stepping aside.

I wanted a place where I could turn and remove myself from the family and be alone. For me, moving forward meant moving to a place of isolation to muster up the strength to walk with everyone. At home, there was the safe haven of my room or the possibility of a solitary early morning walk or bike ride. An introvert with gregarious tendencies, I enjoyed time with people, but I needed time alone to think over how to handle situations. On the boat, I'd been robbed of all of that.

"Sure." Bill's voice softened. I heard him walk away, and soon after, I heard the sound of him wrestling a pot out of the cupboard. Something fell to the floor, the echo bouncing off the close walls. More rustling of packages, some feet shuffling, and another item fell.

I knew Bill wasn't comfortable in the kitchen, and I could picture him pondering where to find things.

I tried to think of what everyone at home in Oregon would be doing on a Saturday. Were the cousins using the trampoline? Did my mom make it to the grocery store every week? But on my bed with my eyes closed, all I could picture was Bill's movement in the galley. Certainly, he was scrambling to think of what to cook. My mind craved silence, but I wasn't going to find it lying down. Letting out a sigh, I sat up and meandered to the galley.

Bill stood with a can in his hand and pulled at the tab. I watched him wrestle it off while I walked toward him.

"Ugh, yuck," I said, seeing the label on the can. "What were you going to do with the Spam?"

"I thought you were napping?" he said as he set the opened can on the counter. "I've got this."

"Are you sure? You sounded like a bull in a china shop from where I was." I picked up the can. "I can't believe you threw this in the grocery cart. Canned meat?" I scrunched up my nose.

"Don't you have a rule in your kitchen?" he questioned and picked up the can and scraped the contents into a frying pan. "Something like, unless you're the cook, you can't complain about the food?"

Chapter 10

"Here"—I reached for the spatula—"let me cook then."

Bill caught my hand and eased it to himself, drawing me close. His voice was quiet. "If you need to rest, go lie down. I can feed the kids."

Searching his blue eyes, I saw the strength of a man who was determined. And I also saw the sliver of disappointment in his flattened lips.

"I want to help," I stated, holding his gaze and watching for affirmation.

He released my hand and took a step back. "Okay." He turned and went to the window, looking out to the bow of the boat where he'd sent the kids.

The twinge in my stomach knotted, reinforcing the guilt I'd held back. Bill and I were a team. How could we move forward if one of us straggled behind?

"I'm sorry." I pushed out the words. "I don't know how to do this."

"Not sure I do either." He opened the door and stepped out.

He needed me. The reminder sank inside me like a rock dropping to the bottom of a clear pool of water, leaving a ripple on the surface. My absence meant he'd carry the load himself. I swallowed the lump in my throat.

From the fridge, I took out an onion and diced it. I figured I'd find a way to make this concoction of spam and potatoes palatable. I also needed to find a way to help Bill move forward, even if I was unhappy.

My inward escape hadn't amounted to anything. *Okay, Bill, I'll set myself aside for the next day, maybe it will help us hurry away from this soured expedition. It hurt so much to see us all floundering with little return for what we'd put in.*

I held Bill's hand and walked along an old logging road on Etolin Island as the kids ran ahead. We'd let out the skiff to ferry ourselves over and explore for the afternoon. The tall trees towered over us, reminding me of the Redwoods in California. Even though it was a bright and sunny day, the trees' canopies filtered the daylight.

"It's beautiful in here." I leaned into Bill, appreciating the time on land to stretch my legs.

"I agree." Bill laughed. "Look at the kids. I don't think I've seen them run that fast in years."

Although banter was teasing, smiles lit their faces as they played chase, zipping across the wide roadway.

Bill brushed off a fallen log and patted the spot next to him. He pulled out the boat ledger and a pen from his coat pocket. "Like I promised."

It was time to tally our gains verses loss after the last few days.

I reached for it and opened it up to the last entry, then I looked up at Bill's face. The numbers didn't add up to much above the red, meaning we'd need to cut our time short. "What do we do?"

"Our goal was to offer our services for six months, but with so little return, we've no choice but to dock and end our business as shrimp tender."

Earlier that morning, the rising sun had warmed my face and the blue sky had invited me to linger in awe of its beauty. Each day I'd pushed forward with the knowledge that I could count down until today, but now that today was here and I saw summer unfold with astounding beauty, I wrestled with

Chapter 10

conflicting emotions. Was I ready for it to end? The green hue on the alders as the buds on their branches sprang to the surface. Shore birds glistened on the beaches, swooping in and out of the shoreline. I couldn't deny the incredible beauty of southeast Alaska.

"I'm sorry it didn't turn out like you wanted." I meant it, I was sad for Bill—for the adventure he sought and the investments we'd made as a family to pursue it. I reached for his hand and gave it a squeeze. Adding to my conflicted feelings was the fact that my happiness about going home was at the expense of his.

"Me too. And I appreciate all that you and the kids did to help. But it's time to let it go." Bill stood up and whistled for the kids. His whistle was cheery, but his defeated expression made my heart ache.

We walked back to the dock and took turns riding in the skiff to the boat, then set our trajectory for the Wrangell City dock.

Dock up, pack up was the mantra we'd chorused with the kids over an early supper. The faster we did both, the quicker we could walk on land and go to Jerry's, a small ice cream shop that doubled as an arcade in downtown Wrangell.

Rayna chanted, "you've got to pack up, pack up so you can dock it, dock it, dock it!"

We laughed at her little dance moves. She waved her arms around and pumped her legs in her oversized, polka-dot rubber boots.

Bill let back on the boat's throttle so we would approach City Harbor at a slower speed. It was the courteous and expected way to enter the harbor, so the boat didn't create a wake and disturb the boats tied at the dock.

"Is that Bail Out?" a voice asked over the radio.

Our kids were on the bow of the boat, huddled in the middle of the deck, anxious to help throw the lines out and tie off.

Bill looked over at me where I stood by the door. He reached for the mic and shook his head at me. He mumbled low and hushed, "What now?" He cued the mic and answered, "Yes, it is. This is Bill Rainer."

"Bill Rainer? Are you aware that your boat is not welcome here because of overdue fees?"

"You're kidding me." I pulled my headband off my head and ran my hands through my greasy hair. Every moment of endurance, of fortitude, to keep on and on, hinged on docking and getting off this cursed boat.

Bill shuffled his feet and shrugged his shoulder. "No sir, can we settle this after we dock? I'm renting this vessel and was unaware of the unpaid invoices."

Oh, God, please, please, just let us get off. I pleaded with God for mercy. We were ready to see it end.

The harbor master countered Bill's plea. "I'll let you dock. Pay the fee, then I'll assign you a slip."

"Thank God," Bill said and shook his head, letting back on the throttle even more and easing the boat into the quiet waters of the main harbor for Wrangell. From there, we could call Steve and have him bring our truck. Life was about to return to normal.

The nostalgia I'd for the beauty of the area wore off like a peeling sunburn. I opened the door and stepped out onto the deck of the boat with the kids, holding back the urge to jump off the edge. I wanted a burger and fries at the local restaurant, a long walk on pavement, and an incredibly long and hot shower. My term as main deck hand on a shrimp tender was officially terminated.

CHAPTER 11

CLUTCHING MY BACKPACK, I LET OUT A QUIET AND deliberate exhale at the sight of my mom's house coming into view. We'd driven all night from the ferry terminal in Bellingham, Washington. I inhaled deeply without the oppression of engulfing moisture and fog from the ocean. Pushing the memory of our last days on the ocean aside, I brushed at the tear forming in my eye, I was nearing home. Everything familiar surrounded me, wrapping me in a soft blanket of warmth, and I never wanted anything to change.

I raised my eyebrows and looked over at Bill. In the low light of the moon shining into the cab of the truck, I saw a smile spread across his tired face. "I'm ready for my own bed," he said.

I pushed my head into the headrest of the seat and closed my eyes. "Yes, and a full night's sleep without having to get up and check the anchor."

Bill started to chuckle, and his laughter shook his shoulders. Shaking his head, he put a hand on his forehead. "You got off the fishing boat so fast, you'd have thought it was on fire."

I joined his amusement over my exit. "You don't appreciate land until you've lived on the water. I couldn't wait." Squinting out the window as we neared my mom's driveway, I saw an unfamiliar vehicle in front of her garage. "I wonder whose car that is?"

"I'm sure your mom has lots to tell you." Bill pulled the Suburban into our long driveway. "Don't forget, I have an interview tomorrow in the afternoon."

"Right." I yawned. "I'll be at mom's tomorrow for a while. I've no clue how long it's been since her banking has been done or her dog has been taken to the vet. I'm sure she'll have a list for me." I twisted in my seat to see if any of the kids were awake. "Hey, I have an idea. Let's leave them here and go inside. They'll find their way in eventually." I undid my seatbelt and grabbed the handle of my door.

"I'll race you for the first shower," he said as he turned off the vehicle. With one swift movement, he'd unlatched his seat belt and bolted for the door.

We laughed at each other and stumbled in the dark for the door handle.

I pushed the wooden front door open, and the familiar smell of our house blasted my senses. I stopped midstride next to the kitchen table.

"Go ahead," I called out to Bill who'd already zipped past me up the stairs, taking them two at a time. Standing in one spot, I let the sight and scent of our home envelope me like an enduring hug. I brushed my hand along the table and moved over to the living room and sat down on the couch. "Home, sweet, home," I said to myself, easing down to lay my head on a decorative pillow I'd placed on the sofa months ago.

So many things were now items of luxury: a couch, pillows, pictures on the wall, a rug on the floor. I didn't even realize how normal and comfortable my life had been before.

A noise caught my attention, and I sat up. There was a beeping sound I hadn't heard when I'd walked in so hurriedly. Tilting my head to the side, I stood up and shook my head at my own haphazard ways. I'd missed the beeping of the answering machine as I'd wafted in my own selfishness of arriving home. I pushed the button on the machine.

"Hi. I hope I have the right number. I'm looking for Grace. This is Amanda, an old friend. Um, give me a call back when you can. I'd love to get together. My number is..." I grabbed a piece of scrap paper near the phone and jotted her number down. What a pleasant surprise. I'd have to make time to see her soon.

The machine beeped again.

"Hey, Grace, Mom said you'd be back this week, and I wanted to touch base with you." It was my older sister Betty's voice. I hadn't heard from her in over a year. "Anyways, I look forward to seeing you over at Mom's. Bye." The machine let out a long beep and went silent.

I stared at the machine. My sister was *here?* At Mom's? Twelve years my senior, she was in a completely different stage of life and seemed to have loads of free time. I'd always wondered why she wasn't a part of caring for our mom. Huh, I guess she'd guilted herself into coming.

Looking around the house, it occurred to me there might be other changes waiting for us. What else would be different? I didn't want the life I left behind tainted with more transitions. I didn't think I could handle it.

THE NEXT MORNING, I PULLED FRESH MUFFINS OUT OF the oven and closed my eyes as I inhaled the sweet, buttery aroma. I'd missed baking so much—and the pleasure of lingering over the preparation of a meal. On the boat, we'd lived by the clock, and it was our taskmaster.

A hutch in the corner of our eating area held some family

heirlooms that I displayed with pride. I opened the cabinet and pulled out a silver tray to place the muffins on and set a tea towel on top of them. *There's no place like home.* I sighed.

I jotted a little note and left it on the counter for the kids to find when they woke up. We'd let them wander into their beds and sleep the day away, but I was headed over to see my mom and take her some homemade baking.

My Birkenstock sandals were by the door where I'd left them months ago. I wore them every time I shuffled next door. I opened the door, and the warm May air was cheery and comfortable. I loved the month of May and the promise of the burst of summer.

As I walked the familiar path, I noted the vehicle I'd seen in front of my mom's place was still there. Ah, that must be my sister's. I walked up the steps and knocked on the screen door and helped myself in like I always did.

"Hi, Momma." I called out, and I heard laughter from down the hall.

"We're back here," Betty called out.

I slipped off my sandals and carried the muffins down the hall to my mom's screened-in porch on the back of the house. She enjoyed this spot at the beginning of the day because it took in the rising sun, and she relaxed on the front porch at the closing of the day to relish in the sunsets.

I entered the porch and saw my sister and mom sitting at the glass-topped table, sipping from teacups. "Hi, Momma." I went right to her and gave her a hug before she could get up.

She grabbed my face in her hands and searched my face. "Oh, you've got stories to tell, I can sense it."

"Hi, honey." My sister Betty got up to greet me with a hug. Her orange-scented perfume tickled my nose, reminding me of the many seasons we'd argued over who would coordinate mom's doctor's appointments. Why she thought she could do it long distance had never made sense to me, but

Chapter 11

she had argued that her years as a secretary made her the best choice.

I placed the silver tray on the table. "It's good to see you. I brought us a little treat." I uncovered the muffins.

"How thoughtful." My mom reached to take one. "So, Gracie girl, tell us all about it."

"Oh, there's not much to say. I'm so happy to be back. I'd rather talk about you and how you've been. And how long have you been here?" I questioned Betty without missing a beat, being sure to turn in my chair to watch her reaction. She'd been my greatest challenge about ten years ago. We'd played a game of tug-of-war with Mom in the middle. I was relieved when she'd finally stepped back and out of the picture.

"Shortly after you left?" She narrowed her eyes and directed her question at Mom. "Does that sound about right?"

Good land, she'd been here all along?

I looked between them, watching my mom smile intently at Betty and then back at me. "I've been well taken care of. Not much new here, just the same ol' thing. We've done some driving around and a little shopping." She reached forward and poured more tea into her bright-pink teacup. But you know me, I'm a homebody. Just watchin' the sun come up and go down. Lovin' every minute of it."

A usual routine sounded very inviting and soothing after a tumultuous time at sea. No place to be and nothing in particular to get done. Even today, there was a massive load of laundry waiting for me, grocery shopping to tackle with Stanna's help—the list went on and on.

"Well, I'm glad you were able to come for such a long time, Betty. What a treat." I pasted a smile on with hopes they didn't see the mask I wore. A shroud to hide my jealousy and guilt. I'd not been a part of their leisurely visits. "But..." I stood up and smoothed my cotton t-shirt. "I've got lots to do, so, I'll come by this evening? We can visit then." I tucked in my chair and touched my mom's hand. "See ya." I flashed a smile and exited the sunroom.

I probably left them with their mouths wide open at my bluntness, but I didn't have time to sit and talk about sugar cubes or honey for tea, nor did I want to discuss the fact that I felt replaced. There was too much in my own life that I needed to address to bring some amount of normalcy to my first day back, like a nice walk, and some time alone.

CHAPTER 12

After dinner, I helped Bill fix a tire on the Suburban that went flat over the course of the day. "I'm so glad this didn't happen on the highway," I said as I handed him the lug nuts.

"No kidding." He twisted the lug nuts on, tightened them, then let the jack down. "Thanks for your help." He looked at his watch. "Don't you have a visit with Amanda at seven?"

"Yes, I'd better head that way." I walked over to the step and grabbed my hoodie. "We're meeting at the trestle bridge, like the old days."

Bill held out his hand to me. "Here's the key."

"Thanks, but I'm going to ride my bike. After being on the boat for so long, I can't wait to exercise my legs." I stood on my tip toes and gave him a kiss. "I'll see ya."

"Bye. Have a good visit." He pocketed the keys as he responded.

I pulled my bike out from beside the house and rode down the gravel road, then a mile past it. I turned toward town where the old bridge stood proud. Amanda and I used to skip along the platform and sing in carefree ways on the way to youth group. A lifetime ago, without a husband, kids, or responsibilities.

It had been a couple of years since we'd seen each other. Amanda had moved down to California, where she and her husband had owned a dairy farm for over twenty years. They'd returned after selling their cattle. I was glad we'd reconnected, since we'd always confided in one another. Our level of friendship always involved raw honesty about our hearts' conditions.

We'd agreed to meet at the picnic area of a state park with a campground situated just before the bridge. I rounded the corner of the first campsite and the wooden pergola came into view. Amanda was waiting on a picnic bench. She stood up and waved when she saw me.

"Hey. It's so good to see you," I said as I hopped off my bike and put down the kickstand. I pulled off my backpack, and we hugged each other tightly.

"I'm so glad it worked out for you to come today, with you just getting back early this morning. My word, how do you do it all?" She sat down and removed her sunglasses from the top of her head. "I'd have napped all day." Her bright smile brought a glow to her whole face. Her dark hair was pulled back in a clip, and I saw a few patches of gray streaking her hairline by her ears.

I waved off her comment. "Nah, too much to do. So, remind me, how long have you been back? How's your family? There's so much to get caught up with." I kicked off my tennis shoes and tucked my feet underneath me on the bench.

"We came back last fall for a couple of weeks but moved back in January. I'd heard you were leaving to go fishing and figured you'd be pretty busy. We're settled in a place close to town, and Jack has a job at the hardware store. He's in charge of contractor sales and visits different job sites. The twins are back from their first year of college." She sighed. "It's a different stage of life now. And you? How old are your kiddos now?"

It'd taken Bill and me a few years to get pregnant, and some of my peers, like Amanda, had their kids right away. Now, their children were out of the house. I couldn't even imagine my life with an empty nest; we were in our busiest of season raising children.

"Stanna is sixteen, Rob is fourteen, and Daniel is twelve. Laura is ten and Rayna is five. I feel like I have a whole baseball team of my own." I shook my head, my eyes wide. "I don't suppose we'd have guessed it'd be me with a Suburban full of kids."

Amanda chuckled. "No, that's for sure. So, what's the scoop with fishing? You going back after a break?"

"No, we're done. Bill has an interview this afternoon in town."

We chatted for well over an hour, and the thoughts I had about my youth group experience when we first viewed the boat came back around. I wanted to weigh Amanda's impressions of it all alongside my own.

I cleared my throat and leaned closer to Amanda. "I've been waiting to tell you about something that happened before we started fishing."

She pulled out Chapstick and rolled it on her lips. "Sure."

"The boat we rented reeked of this horrible musty smell, and my memory journeyed back to the youth group trip, when—" I cleared my throat again. "Well, you remember."

She searched my face with her bright blue eyes. "I do. I haven't thought about that in a long time. Now that you mention it, when I do think about it, I feel an uneasy twinge of emotion that I can't quite explain."

"I know. It hit me so hard I couldn't even think or pay any attention to the boat. I didn't realize how it had molded me." I pulled my bandana off my head and unfolded it.

Amanda narrowed her eyes. "What do you mean?"

"Like how no one believed us." My heart started pounding at the memory. "Why couldn't they trust us? Why'd they believe the leader over us? It still makes me mad."

Amanda reached into her large leather purse and pulled out a small notebook. "I had a different response." She placed her palm on the table. "I know what you're saying, but hear me out. We could have been put in a more vulnerable situation, but God provided a way of escape. Nothing happened to any of the girls in the tent." She drew a circle on the paper. "I've always looked back and reminded myself there will be many times in our relationship with God where we will be threatened from our circle of safety." At the top of the page, she formed some arrows pointing down at the circle. "We have to be aware of the times we are weak in our faith. Are we believing lies? Is our vision clouded? I was reminded to guard myself with the power of prayer. God kept us safe that night. Don't ever forget He is with you."

I appreciated the picture my dear friend formed on the page and also in my mind. It had been easy to focus on the response of others instead of thanking God for His protection. "Thanks, for helping redirect my thoughts." I pointed at the drawing she'd made. "Huh, looks like arrows being shot at a target."

Amanda smiled, picked up her pen and drew a dot in the center of the circle. "Yes, I see that too. Or we can look at it a bit differently and see the circle as a shield, knowing God is our shield to fend off those fiery arrows." She drew flames on the arrow tips.

"I love word pictures like this. A good reminder to show my kids, too," I stated as I tied my bandana back on.

"Not to get preachy with you, but remember the saying I told you about with my new career writing women's fiction? Show don't tell. As parents, we can talk and talk until we are blue in the face, but we need to show our kids how we live out our faith."

Another good reminder. I'd sunk so deep into my own doubts and fears while we were on the tender. "I deserve an F on that one lately. It's like the boat we rented was cursed or something. We couldn't do anything right. In my heart, I believed we'd fail. My actions showed my disbelief." I put my hand on my forehead and rested my elbows on the table. "I wasn't a very good example of how to weather doubt." I watched Amanda put her sunglasses back on and reposition herself on the bench seat. Did she have more wisdom to share?

"Shake the dust off those boots and move on, my friend. Speaking of which, I need to get back home." She motioned toward my bike, propped against a tree. "Want to throw your bike in the back of my truck and let me give you a ride?"

"Oh, thanks for the offer but I enjoyed my ride here so much, and I need the exercise." I waved off the suggestion and reached for her hand on the table. "I appreciate your friendship and willingness to speak truth to me. Let me know how I can be praying for you."

Amanda gave my hand a squeeze, rose from her seat and placed her hands in the pockets of her light-purple sweatshirt. "It's a new season of life for me. Pray I use my time wisely." She pulled her keys from her pocket. "Want to meet again in a couple of days when we both have more time?"

I stood up and walked toward my bike. "Sounds good to me. Just give me a call and let me know what works for you."

"Okay, talk to you soon." She opened her truck door, kicked her feet together to loosen any dirt from the parking lot off her shoes, and shut the door. Her habit of shaking the dust off her boots was a ritual she'd acquired from her dairy farming days. I noted it was ingrained in her, and I should likewise learn to form a similar pattern in my own thinking, like moving on graciously from difficult circumstances.

Pedaling my bike, I savored the scenery and atmosphere of my stomping grounds. I'd wandered these roads as a little girl, a teenager, and a young woman; whether it was walking, biking, or driving, I knew this space with my eyes closed. So many memories were created on these paths, and I looked forward to years of embracing more. I rounded the corner and sprinted to our driveway.

Bill was out in the yard, pushing the seed spreader on the front lawn. I saw the white specks of fertilizer dispersing from the bottom.

I stopped short of the grass, waved, and got off my bike, walking it along the sidewalk. "Hey," I said.

"Hey back," Bill said. "Let me finish this row, then we'll walk a lap around the yard." Bill continued his straight line to the edge of the yard.

I brushed my hands through my windblown hair, then repositioned my red paisley bandana on my head. I looked around the yard and saw the kids were in the back, playing with the dogs. Our friends who'd housed our pets must have returned them after I'd left.

"I've missed our walks," I said as I approached Bill.

He grabbed my hand in his and swung it at his side. "Me too. How was your visit with Amanda?"

"Great. It's always the same with her, like we press pause on our friendship and then resume where we left off." I gazed at the sky, which displayed orange and red hues off in the distance.

"Those friendships are a gift. Speaking of treasures, I wanted to let you in on a deal I came across this evening." Bill let go of my hand and dug into his pants pocket.

"Oh?" I was curious about what he referred to and imagined it was a different vehicle since the Suburban recently crested two hundred thousand miles.

"Let me read it word for word here so I don't get it mixed up. A seventy-six-foot steel, gulf shrimper, located in Wrangell, and the asking price is negotiable based on a recent boat appraisal. Hm, my guess is it might have an engine that needs replacing." Bill looked at the paper and then at me with questioning eyes.

"Is this a joke?" I stepped back from him, searching his face,

Chapter 12

eyes and ears for any clue—some movement or twitch alerting me he was pulling my leg. His appearance didn't falter.

"No, it's not." He lightly shook his head and folded the paper.

"What about the interview? Aren't we back home to dig our roots in deeper here?" I shook my head and the skin on my back tingled with discomfort.

"The interview wasn't a good fit." He tucked the paper back in his pocket. "You know I'm not a quitter. I've got to try fishing again. I didn't take the time to enjoy the salt air and feel the breeze on my face, and now that I'm here, I'm itching to go back."

Time seemed to slow down as we neared the memory stones nestled under the trees. Would I be able to hold myself up under the weight of this thought to return to the Alaska waters? "I, uh, don't feel the same way." I struggled to find the right words. I knew Bill was aware of the discomfort I'd experienced in Alaska.

"We all struggled, but this wouldn't be the same. We'd own our boat, call the shots, and start with a blank slate. When you purchase a vessel, you name it yourself, leaving any rumors behind. We can do this. I saw an immense amount of fortitude in my family, pushing against all odds." Bill motioned to Mom's adjacent yard. "And your mom has help now. You won't have to worry about her."

In one breath of a season, I'd been displaced as my mom's helper, and become a primary crew member on a commercial fishing vessel.

Bill stopped and placed his strong hands on my shoulders. "I'm sorry you didn't see this coming. The dream of living on the water and working for ourselves is an invitation hard to shake."

I needed to sit down and brace myself for all the questions reeling through my thoughts. "Can we go inside and map this out a bit? I'm not following what you're saying." I shook my head in denial of what Bill was implying. I pulled away from his touch and walked to the house.

The only morsel of thanksgiving that rose in my heart as I reached the door was that Bill wanted me to be a part of his dreams. However, if this suggestion had pounced on me like a wild mountain lion while we were dating, I was certain I'd have run away.

CHAPTER 13

I SLEPT IN THE NEXT DAY AND PULLED THE COVERS UP and around my head as I woke. The bright light peeked across the room through the slit in the curtains, streaming on the bed next to Bill's empty spot. It was unlike me to rest past my usual time. I loved and savored my morning routine. However, when the alarm sounded, I briskly knocked it off my bedside table. My stomach had churned all night after hearing Bill's notion to return to Alaska and reclaim his reputation and dream. All I wanted to do was bury the idea under a large pile of fresh soil and plant a new sapling. A seed that would yield a fruitful crop for all of us, where I'd have room to stretch out and have space for me.

I rolled over, turning my back to the light and to the notion of returning north. Should I push back at Bill, my faithful man who loved me fiercely and provided for our family? He didn't want to give up. He wanted to save face and redeem our disgraceful exit.

I'd heard of marriages nearing rocky shorelines and battling the winds to survive. Were Bill and I in danger of dashing against a jagged edge that would pierce the protective cocoon of a twenty-three-year-long commitment?

I stretched out in bed and rubbed my forehead. "Ugh, I've got to get up," I said aloud. Maybe after some coffee I'd take a short walk and clear my clouded thinking and regain some normalcy. Could I have one day that resembled what I use to have? Was it too much to ask?

Easing out of bed, I wiggled my toes and looked around our room. I'd missed my creature comforts and routine so much. How had I become such a creature of habit that when life veered away from the usual, I'd plummeted? Now that I was back home, I wanted to bask in the peace it normally brought me and have time to sort my thoughts—maybe journal a little bit and find my bearings.

I took my time picking out some clothes and tidying my room before taking a long shower. I closed the door to my room and smiled. "It's the simplest things that bring me sanity." I spoke aloud to myself.

A note on the kitchen table answered my question of why the house was so quiet. Stanna had taken all the kids to their cousin's house, and they'd return in the afternoon.

Feeling refreshed from my shower, I poured myself a cup of coffee and went to sit on the front step. Bill mentioned running some errands in the first part of the day, and I was thankful for the peace within the yard and house.

Just like before, it all changed. The thought steamed out like the blow from a whale's spiracle. Predictable times of quiet, a steady pace to the day, scheduled visits with family; it all flowed with ease and comfort. The rhythm of life I'd set aside when we'd left for Wrangell proved to have invigorated me in the past.

I set my cup on the step and stood up, my bare feet gripping the wooden stairs. The sun shone on my face, and I closed my eyes, savoring the warmth. How had I become such a creature of habit that I'd lost my way on a short stint away from home? Why did the rays on my cheeks feel so different? So refreshing?

Chapter 13

"Is that you, Gracie girl?" I heard my mom call out.

Startled, my stance on the stairs buckled, and I reached to hold the railing.

"Hey, Momma." I spoke without a glance and opened the screen door to reach for my Birkenstocks. Pushing my feet in them, I picked up my mug and set it on the railing before walking across my yard to where my mom stood on her front porch.

Her smile faded when I came closer. "Uh-oh. What's going on?"

How did she read my soul with such a brief glance?

"What?" I questioned, hoping to draw a veil in place and plead innocence.

"C'mon in and tell me. Your sister is gone shopping." She turned to reach for her front doorknob. "You didn't come last night. I've been worried about you." She glanced over her shoulder, concern in her narrowed green eyes.

Shoot. I'd completely forgotten. How had I let it slip? As a rigid list-maker and project-oriented individual, it was uncommon for me to miss a meeting, show up late, or not visit someone as promised. "Sorry, I've got to get back in the swing of things. I guess I can't call it jet lag, but I feel pretty tired." There wasn't a lie woven in my statement.

Her nod revealed that she believed me, and she reached out her arms for a hug.

"I missed you," I said, breathing in her floral fragrance and the wave of comfort holding her brought.

"I missed you too, baby girl. Now come on in for some sweet tea and tell me all about the haunted boat that robbed you of your enthusiasm for life." She moved forward through the door, holding it open for me.

Again, she'd pried an opening and exposed the wound I tried to hold inside.

I didn't respond, but followed her lead to the front room where she often sat to read. She'd already placed a pitcher and some glasses on a wooden coffee table like she was expecting me.

"What makes you say that?" I asked as I crossed my legs and placed one of her under-stuffed decorative couch pillows behind my back.

"God," she stated without any explanation, then poured herself a glass of the amber tea she'd made in a large mason jar out in the sun. The years must have taught her how to linger with one word and let it steep like tea in a cup. "I prayed for you every day. God impressed upon me to pray often, so I determined it must be tryin' for you." She sipped her tea and tipped the glass to me. "Want some?"

I waved at her. "I just finished my coffee, but thanks."

"Yesterday, your face answered every question I've pondered. It was rough for you, and then you returned to find things all upturned. I know you." She leaned forward and shook her finger at me with a smile on her bright red lips. "You don't like that. Nope, not my Gracie girl." She shrugged. "I made up the haunted part for effect. But the flash of your eyes tells me there might be some truth to it." Momma leaned back with a slow look of satisfaction on her face and folded her hands on her lap.

I let my shoulders rest back into the couch. "I'm not very good at holding my cards tight. Good thing I'm not a gambler." I smiled and shrugged. "It wasn't my cup of tea, per se. And yes, the boat itself was a challenge since the owner has a horrible reputation and we couldn't shake it. As much as it bothered me, I know it hurt Bill more than any of us because he wanted to prove we could succeed."

Momma rubbed her eyes with her hand and blinked. "Sounds rough. There were times when I watched your dad struggle, and it was no fun. I sense there's more to the story. Are the kids okay?"

"The kids are great. It's that Bill wants to go back." I pushed the words out and let them sit out in the open for my mom to interpret however she may. Would she offer wise counsel, nod in approval, or give me a blank stare?

Her affect didn't alter, and she searched my face. Perhaps she was waiting for me to tell her what I thought?

"Ah, I sense the winds of change are blowing hard," she said, finally. "And what will Grace do? Will she stand with the wind at her face or turn her back?" She used her hands to brace herself and inched forward in her chair. "What did God impress upon your heart when you asked Him?"

I fidgeted with my wedding ring as a thickness formed in my throat. I replayed my mom's words about the wind and her question about my response. How was I reacting? I hadn't bowed in prayer or taken any time to form words in my mind or heart petitioning the Lord. Instead, I'd found solace in the softness of my bed and the quiet of my house. I stared down, swallowed hard, and returned my gaze to my mom. "I haven't prayed about it yet. Bill told me about a boat last evening."

Momma nodded her head. *Did she sense I was making excuses?*

"I tell you what," she said. "Let's pray about it right now and hand it over to Him. Okay?"

I shifted my position on the couch and nodded.

My mom reached for my hand, and I grasped her thin, warm fingers. "Dear Heavenly Father, we come to You now asking for wisdom for Bill and Grace. Direct their steps and help Grace as she swallows the past and looks to what You have for her in the future. Thank You for preserving them from harm while in Wrangell and bringing them back safely. Help them both to cling to You and Your word always, No matter where they are, You are the anchor for their souls. In Jesus name I pray, amen."

At the word amen, I felt my heart reach a steady and calm pace instead of the pounding force it had when I'd first woke up. "Thanks, Momma."

"Now, pour yourself some tea. Heaven knows you need some sugar to get yourself up and take on the day. Boat or no boat, it doesn't matter. What matters is in here." She tapped her finger over her sternum.

I still held her frail hand in mine, and I gave it a squeeze. "I love you." I said, looking into her eyes that held a strength and dignity I'd long admired.

I let go of her hand and poured myself a glass of her special homemade sun sweet tea with a hint of orange.

She was right. I knew the recipe and the ingredients I needed to move forward. However, I'd have to choose to pull them out, measure them with precision, and watch the combination transform when mixed together.

Together with Bill, our prayers to God would shine the light on his desire to return to Alaska. My own selfish thoughts had pushed God out of my days, and I'd lost my grip on what'd been my anchor, just as Momma said.

IN THE EVENING, BILL SPREAD NAUTICAL CHARTS ON our large wooden kitchen table. Rob, Daniel, and Laura listened carefully as their dad went over names of islands and coves of the Pacific waters in southeast Alaska.

I sat on the couch with Rayna as she read from her early readers, practicing the first-grade work she needed to complete before the end of the month. We'd set aside schoolwork while fishing, and now it was time to regain momentum before the busyness of summer swamped us. Rayna read with her finger under the word she was sounding out. One last child to climb the mountain of learning to read.

Chapter 13

"Mom, what's this one say again?" she asked as she pointed to the *ph* consonant blend.

"It makes the sound of an F. I know that seems weird and is probably hard to remember. But you'll get it." I gave her a side hug and pulled her in close. Not my baby anymore, I enjoyed her cuddles on the couch while they lasted, knowing when she was twice this age, she might not want to do much with me. Like Laura, who'd been my sidekick for years and now drifted toward spending time with her older brothers and competing with them. It was all good. It was supposed to happen that way. But I wanted to freeze this happy moment of us growing together in my mind.

"Thanks, Mom," Rayna said, taking in a deep breath before she continued on. The intense appearance of her furrowed brow revealed the level of concentration she poured into learning so she could read like the *big* kids.

Could we move together as one unit toward a family goal? Bill believed we already were. I wasn't so sure. I also wasn't so sure it was the wisest or safest aspiration to include all of us in the new endeavor. I still shivered, remembering Rob swinging out on the boat rigging over the open water. The concept of a dangerous sea and the respect it demanded were obviously overlooked by most of my kids.

Risk was only one factor in the equation, though. The algebraic rules of one step before another reminded me that we were still new to the business.

Bill folded the charts and cleared his throat. "Let's all sit in the living room." His familiar nod toward me told me that he wanted to share something important.

I fidgeted with my wedding band, acutely aware of the empty feeling in my stomach. What plan had he conjured up? I was certain that for most of the day his mind had formulated parts and pieces to the puzzle of succeeding at commercial fishing. He was my determined man. I loved him for it, and I bordered on protesting it. He held my views in high regard. If I had fully objected to his vision, he would have reconsidered. But what would I replace it with? I had no goal or vision to promote instead. He wasn't standing in the way of a career I wanted. I only ever wanted to be a part of his, and he knew that. I just wished he'd chosen something that didn't take us far away from comfort and safety. He stood erect with his shoulders pulled back, and his strong frame towered over the rest of us who were sitting down. The confidence he held was admirable, and it stunned me how he'd grabbed onto this idea with such exuberance.

"As you know, we left Wrangell with a bitter taste in our mouths," he said. "It's no secret it didn't turn out how we planned. But if this is something I'm going to do for a career, we're going to have to start over and try again. This time though, your mom and I are considering buying our own boat."

Bill continued on, explaining the benefits of ownership while I swallowed the lump in my throat at the thought of being in debt for such a large sum of money. The kids didn't have any idea what kind of a weight this represented. Their dad wanted to start a new career in his early fifties and relocate his growing family to the ocean.

I tucked my feet in, crisscrossed, where I sat. The image in my mind was more like me reeling in a hundred-pound halibut with the words *not for me* tagged on its belly. This was Bill's dream, Bill's plan, and I was an onlooker. But I agreed with Momma's prayer for wisdom, and her advice to let the past go and look to the future. I wanted a new image in my mind.

"Anyone have any questions or thoughts?" Bill asked as he picked up the charts from the table and rolled them up, placing a rubber band around them to hold them in place.

"What kind of a timeline are we working with?" Stanna asked. She'd positioned herself with an open posture, arms

Chapter 13

unfolded, ready to listen. I appreciated her tendency to be compliant. Hers was a good question.

"There are a number of openers, and your mom and I will have to determine first if this is what we're going to pursue." Bill paused and looked directly at me, questioning me with his eyes. "If we do, then I assume we'd need to leave by fall and get ready for the openers that start in October. Then we'd play a little game of journeying from one open fishing area to the next. We'd fish into the winter."

"I've got a question," Rob piped up. "What would we do this time?"

Another good question I'd pondered myself. There'd need to be more of a schedule, and the kids would have schoolwork. What did Bill envision? I watched his face carefully, hoping each little prod might deter his movement forward.

"Excellent question." Bill rubbed his hands together as a light-hearted smile spread across his flushed face. "You'll have schoolwork to do, overseen by your mom." He motioned toward me with his hand. "You'll all be deckhands, helping with the shrimp pots. There will be gear this time. We won't be tenders, but fishermen. There will be lots and lots of work to do." He looked down at his feet while he shuffled them and set his gaze on Stanna. "I have a job specifically for you. There's a whole lot of paperwork with this one. I'll need someone to help read all the fish and game regs and sort out the dos and don'ts. With your attention to detail, I think you can keep us straight."

Bill had truly formed a plan. He'd thought it through—maybe while we were out before on the ocean, learning from his mistakes, imagining what he could do differently to make it a success. How it could all look different. He didn't see the *not for me* sign that I did. He saw an *open for business* sign.

Stanna smiled at her dad and looked over at me.

My family was rallying, and I was stalling. They were gaining momentum, and I was lagging behind. I had a deep-seated need to unravel my heart and expose the willful dislike I felt for this continuation to Alaska. I wanted to escape the idea—throw all the planning overboard. The tug-of-war boiled in me like warm waters from a hidden natural hot spring, trickling out of the depths of the rocks.

If everyone else was eager to go back and face the challenge with determination and resolve, why couldn't I cheer us on?

CHAPTER 14

A COUPLE OF WEEKS LATER, I MET WITH AMANDA FOR a cup of coffee at a sandwich shop. I'd brought a small notebook and my Bible, knowing I could draw from her insight and help for my heart's response to Alaska.

The idea of escaping the whole notion of the family working on a boat grew with time. Could I find a reason for Bill to go ahead alone, and the kids and I to come later? Perhaps then he'd wait longer to go and eventually decide not to. The deadline to pull the trigger loomed over us.

Amanda sat outside at a glass-topped table under an umbrella that shaded her from the hot sunshine. I waved as I walked down the sidewalk toward her. "Hey there." I pulled the chair out across from her and sat down.

"Hi, friend," she said. "I'm so glad it worked out for us to meet. I already ordered you an iced coffee, my treat." She pulled her dark curls up into a ponytail and waved at her flushed face. "Phew, it's a hot one today already."

"It sure is. Thanks." I placed my notebook and Bible on my lap.

"So, what's new with you?" She leaned forward in her chair to position herself more fully in the shade.

"I'm really stuck. And I mean really, really stuck." I leaned my elbows on the table.

"Uh-oh what now? I hope your mom is okay?" Amanda took off her sunglasses and searched my eyes.

"No, no, it's not her. It's me. I'm in a rut, and I don't know how to get out." I pulled my Bible from my lap and set it on the table. "Bill. wants to go back to Alaska. This time as boat owners, fishing for shrimp. He wants to leave ASAP and I want to run the other direction."

Amanda nodded and bit at her top lip. "Hm."

"I trust Bill and all, and I want to work alongside him. I love that part of our life. But I'm not interested in fishing. It seems like it all went wrong, and I couldn't even escape myself, never mind everyone else—being all cooped up in a small space like that." I pulled my headband off and unwrapped it, gave it a shake off to the side and hung it on the back of my chair.

"What does Bill say to all of this?"

"I'm not saying it all to him. Part of me wants to, the other part doesn't. I feel so selfish when I don't do whatever everyone else wants. It's a war inside of me. I know if Bill sets his mind to it, he will do well in most anything. But maybe *I* don't want to do well at this." I hung my head in my hands. "I don't know. I was an impatient mess with the last venture."

The waitress brought our iced coffees with whipped cream on top in tall glasses and set them on the table. "Thanks, Jill," Amanda said. She took a sip of her drink. "G-R-A-C-E. It's an acronym for God's Riches at Christ's Expense. Have you ever heard that?"

I sipped my sweet coffee and shook my head. My curiosity was pricked as to how it related to my situation.

"You are a testimony of the grace of God. We don't deserve all He's given us. All His richest blessings are poured out to us! Do you doubt He will supply all your needs?"

"Oh? I hadn't thought of it that way." I wiped a dab of

Chapter 14

whipped topping from my upper lip and chuckled at the thought of how it looked.

Amanda laughed along with me and handed me a napkin.

"How do you do that all the time? Slam me back to reality." I sipped my coffee.

"Wow, *slam* sounds harsh." Raising her eyebrows, she continued. "You are diligent and courteous." She held out her hand and pointed at her fingers, counting out qualities with each fingertip. "And enthusiastic, disciplined, highly observant, kind, intelligent, and unselfish. I see a very talented friend sitting in front of me." She repositioned herself and leaned closer.

I picked up my headband and fumbled it in my hands, looking at Amanda. "But when things went awry, I crumbled. What does that say about me?"

"Nothing." She answered matter-of-factly, spinning her glass on the table. "It means there was a bullseye on you. And it means the evil one wants to devour you. He's looking for the vulnerable, to rip at any thread of your relationship with God. When he sees an opening, he attacks." She reached for my Bible and pulled it closer to her. "Now, let's make a battle plan so the next time you face a fear of the unknown you'll be ready to escape the lies."

Amanda opened the Bible to a familiar passage, and I took note of the verses.

"You need to lay claim to your life and memorize these," Amanda said. "Maybe put them on a three-by-five card and tuck them in your Bible to read *every* morning." She reached for her purse, pulled out an oversized pencil, and began shading on the paper. "I'll doodle something for you to help drive the point home."

Leaning forward, I watched her sketch. When she was finished, I turned the paper and looked at her drawing of a simple mask.

"You'll have to help me understand." I said with a chuckle, uncertain how it connected.

"In the jungles, people will place a mask on the back of their head so that if a wild animal tries to attack them from behind, they'll see a face and not overtake them." She clasped her hands. "Isn't that brilliant?"

The verse acted as masks to deter the prowling enemy. Could I formulate a similar guard in my own life? "Interesting idea. How about you come with me to Wrangell? Then we could meet all the time and you'd help me?"

Amanda shook her head, and her ponytail fell out. She rolled her eyes at her hair. Her long curls were her trademark, and she worked to keep them pulled back, especially in the heat. "That's a fun idea. But I'm sure the answer is probably no."

I snapped my fingers. "Shucks."

She reached for my hand. "You can join Bill in Alaska or anywhere, as long as your heart is in tune with the truth of God."

Her words mirrored what Momma had tried to tell me earlier: it was a matter of the heart.

I folded my headband and smoothed out the wrinkles, then wrapped it around my head. "You know what they say, 'north to Alaska, north to the future.'"

Amanda formed a kind smile across her blushed face. "Yup, and don't forget what your name means. G-R-A-C-E, you have a wealth of help from your Heavenly Father. He has your future in His hands."

The childhood song came to mind of God having the whole world in His hands. Could my heart say yes to Alaska, remembering God was with me there, ready to lavish us with His help?

Chapter 14

ONCE I GREETED BILL WITH A TENTATIVE YES TO pursue buying the boat he relentlessly began planning. Determined to have our shrimp pots in the water by mid-October, he planned out each day at home.

In late August, he traveled ahead of us on the ferry to work on overhauling the boat. The steel vessel we'd bought was a seventy-six-foot gulf shrimper, and Bill would turn it into what we needed, adding a living area and bunk beds.

While he was bursting at the seams to get started, I could certainly wait for a very long time for it all to begin. I couldn't lie about how I felt about it, but I was still going. I'd have to set my mind to be watchful for doubts and resist the lies the enemy told me.

The night before he left, I shook my head and smiled at him. "My wild, Alaskan man," I said as I gave him a hug. "There's no stopping you, is there?"

"I'm antsy cause there's a lot of work there for me to do." He leaned down and stroked my hair. "And yes, I can hardly wait."

The kids and I followed him weeks later, flying commercially to Alaska instead of going on the ferry like last time. I felt like royalty on the jet, eating a meal at thirty-thousand feet instead of having to travel for days along the coast on the marine highway. The kids took pictures of one another with the pilot when we landed in Ketchikan, the last stop on the "milk run" before Wrangell. From Seattle, the plane made flights to the remote cities of southeast Alaska on its way north to Anchorage.

The plane touched down on the island and taxied to the small terminal. I leaned over Daniel to get a glimpse out the window. The mountains to the east were dark green, contrasting with the bright-blue, late-September sky. With the runway next to the ocean, I couldn't help but notice the glassy water dazzling in the bright light of midday. A strange sense of breathlessness caught in my throat; it appeared inviting.

The kids were laughing beside me, and the excitement of the moment gave me a sense of camaraderie. We'd arrived to help propel Bill's dream into motion.

I leaned into Daniel's shoulder. "What do ya think?"

His blue eyes sparkled back at me. "I've never seen it over on this side of the island before. And this airplane ride was more like flying in a rocket." A wide grin spread across the ruddy complexion of his face. "How about you?"

His question startled me. I raised my eyes, searching for the right answer. How did I feel? "I'm hopeful things will be much better this time." I patted his shoulder, then watched the kids on the other side of the plane gather their few items from under the seats.

The airport was small, and we exited, walking out of the plane and over to the terminal. The fresh, briny air welcomed me like the brush of a velvet blanket. I inhaled deeply and smiled as I watched the kids hurry to the terminal entrance.

Thank You, Lord, for a safe trip. Help me to ride this wave of elation and not let it snuff out in the slightest breeze.

I waited for my turn to greet Bill, who was smothered in embraces from the kids when we walked in. His eyes met mine, and he raised his eyebrows as though asking, *So?*

"Okay, let me give your mom a hug." He reached for me.

"Hi," I said before I reached up and gave him a kiss. "It's so good to be here." The words fell out without a thought. Did I mean that? Or did I sense the excitement of the moment?

He put his arm around me and drew me to him. We walked in step over to the tiny baggage claim, which wasn't more than fourteen feet wide. A small ramp extended down the side of the wall to hold the luggage as it dropped into a blocked-off compartment. "Oh, it's so great to have you all here. I missed you guys," Bill stated as he gave Rob a gentle jab on the shoulder.

Rayna started to bounce in place. "Daddy, what color is our new boat?"

"It's a shiny silver." Bill gave her ponytail a little tug. "And boy, do I ever need your help in getting some things ready for all those shrimp we're going to have."

"Oh, fun." Her exclamation squealed out of her tiny frame.

"Grab your bags," Bill called out as we held hands down the slanted walkway to the door. "I missed you," he whispered to me.

"I missed you too." I smiled at him. Pride welled in me at the sight of him and the peace I saw on his face to have his plans unfolding.

"You'll never guess what I named her." Bill said as he opened the door for me.

"Her?" I asked as I place my purse on the seat and turned to him, watching his eyes dance in the summer light.

"Our ship. I named it Amazing Grace." He picked me up and swirled me in the air.

"Aw." I beamed at him and gave him a peck on the cheek. Seeing him nudged my building hopefulness for the adventure forward and reminded me of how much he loved us.

We picked up a few groceries from the store and drove over to the dock, where the kids ran ahead down the ramp.

"Just wait until you see the girl. It'll feel like home." Bill offered his sentiment as he reached to take the bags out of the small cartful of supplies he'd pushed to the boat.

"Sure." My reply was more of a reflex as the reality of our arrival impressed itself upon me. An odd sense of joy mixed with hesitation and the feeling that it couldn't be real.

But it was. We were actually doing this.

We worked together to take items onto the sparkling boat tied off in the City Harbor.

"Here." Bill reached his hand out to me and helped me climb in while the kids scurried around the deck like a pinball machine at the arcade. "Let me show you around."

I breathed a silent prayer. *Lord, don't let me hate it.* I didn't want to loathe the sight or smell of any part of it. Bill tugged me along and showed me the features of the rigging and pulleys, which all made a whole lot more sense to him than it did to me. I nodded approvingly. "I'm sure it will mean more when I see it in motion."

We skirted the game of tag the kids had exploded into and went inside. *Let it not smell musty, please, please,* my thoughts chanted in my head. There was no room for me to be swallowed whole again by a distant memory I'd come to terms with.

"See." Bill held out his hand, pointing to the galley. His gaze turned from the kitchen to me, and he gave me a pleading smile.

"Wow," I blurted out, as I moved closer to the stark-white, sterile-looking counters and cupboards. I'd never thought I'd be blinded by the brightness of a cooking area. I rubbed my hand on a cutting board hanging on a hook; it also was white.

The log home back in Oregon was inviting. The soft tones of amber, aged walls, and our brown furniture were comforting features of the house we'd built. I'd accented the kitchen with hues of delightful teal-blue, adding a cheery tone to the room. This kitchen was strikingly different. Nothing about it felt the same as the one I'd left behind. Nothing.

Bill bumped his shoulder against mine with a nudge. "Here, I'll show you the bunk room."

I followed him through a maze to the forecastle where he'd built bunks to frugally occupy the space designated for sleeping only. "You did a nice job." I rubbed my hand on the sturdy structure and noted the lighting he'd added close to the heads of the beds. "Where do we sleep?"

Chapter 14

He grasped my hands in his. "You, my dear, have walked right past it. It's in the stateroom."

Unclear about what he meant, I shrugged my shoulders and followed him back in the direction we'd come from to a small room tucked in near the kitchen. The living space, kitchen, and bedroom together were about sixteen feet by ten feet. I stepped in ahead of Bill in hopes that my first impression was incorrect. A twin bed filled the space. I gulped back at the memory of our queen bed back home. "Cozy." I turned and faced Bill, raising my eyebrows. "This is very, very different from the last boat." I tried to sound matter-of-fact, and perhaps I was only comparing one to the other and not to the dream-home I'd locked up tight less than twenty-four hours ago. Perhaps I should search for five positive aspects of the new boat to appreciate?

"I'm so glad you aren't upset this time." Bill wrapped me in a hug.

Help me, God. Help me to roll with things and find somewhere to call my own.

My prayer was interrupted by a call from the kids shouting out for Bill and me.

The familiar world I'd lived in was gone. Everything about my life was changing. Everything. There was no stopping the pounding in my heart, the cry for the safety net of my former everyday life.

CHAPTER 15

IN HOPES OF SHOWING BILL THAT I WAS SAYING *YES* TO his Alaska dream, I decided to decorate the space and make it feel more like a home. I dug out some of the sea glass I'd collected and glued it together, making a wreath. I tied some thread to it and hung it on a suction cup hook we had on the window for a thermometer. I stood back and appreciated the teal-blue colors mixed with green accenting the white kitchen. Next, I placed the colorful dish rags I'd knitted onto the counter. "There. A splash of color." I smiled at the space and rubbed my hand on the counter. I wanted to warm up to the area since over the last couple of weeks on the boat, I'd managed to snap at almost every high moment my family celebrated—not exactly the person I aimed to be.

Rubbing my temples, I opened my eyes and read the verse on the card I'd colored and put on the fridge that morning. I read it out loud. "Thou wilt keep him in perfect peace, whose mind is stayed on thee: because he trusteth in thee." The verse from Isaiah settled on my soul like the calm touch of a mom on her upset baby in the middle of the night.

I thought of what my life used to be, the freedoms I'd taken for granted. I opened my Bible to the spot I'd marked with

Amanda and pulled out the three-by-five card we'd jotted verses on.

These are for my new life.

Shocked at the thought passing through my mind, I closed my eyes tight. I needed to have the right frame of mind and capture the negative pulsations that drove me down to a deep, dark place.

The fact didn't change that it was a new reality and rhythm that demanded my part. Try as I might, I couldn't keep my negative feelings from spilling over. I received shocked looks from the kids when I complained to Bill and the terse tone in my instructions to them shocked me.

I live my life on a boat.

Unsure of why I needed to remind myself of this obvious element, I wrote it down on the card. Was God impressing a truth upon me? I clicked my pen and tucked it next to my notebook on the table and, barely above a whisper, reread the verse in hopes I'd have it memorized by that evening.

"Mom?"

I looked up to see Rob peeking his head in the doorway.

"Yeah?"

"Dad says he needs your help with something."

"Okay." I closed my Bible and stood up.

Someone always needs help with something. Shoot, I just did what I didn't want to do. *Sheesh, Grace.*

Steer me, Lord. Steer my heart. 'Cause I can't.

I found Bill tinkering with some contraption.

"Here." He handed me some pliers.

I stood in silence and looked out at the gray water. The fall tides were swelling, and we'd noticed the changes more so the last few days. Our boat named Amazing Grace jounced with a wave, and I stumbled in place. "Whoa." I reached out for something to hold onto, but nothing was within reach, except Bill. I rested my hand on his shoulder as he crouched over his project.

"Come closer so I can show this to you." Bill pulled me down to his level. "If something was ever to happen to me, you'd need to know this, okay?"

Good grief. This wasn't helping my goal for a positive train of thought. "Okay, maybe you should show Rob too," I offered.

"I already have. I know you want to pass the buck to him, but I need you to be aware in case he forgets."

"All right," I answered as I watched Bill go over a sequence of steps that were of utmost importance. It only solidified in my mind how out of sync I was with the new normal. Here it was, the stark contrast of where I'd come from and where I was going. Before life on a boat, I'd never had to learn the mechanics of a machine or system. If anything, I was a master at understanding people. I squinted my eyes and tried to make sense of what he was explaining.

Bill straightened, standing solidly. He set his jaw, pressed his lips firmly together and grunted. "Go on inside. I need to pull anchor, and we'll head over to Walker Cove to set pots before high tide."

It was obvious to us all that Bill had set his sights high. He wanted to fish every opener and pull as many shrimp as possible.

As I went inside, I felt a familiar nip at the back of my neck. The weather was changing, and maybe there was more to anticipate than a high tide.

The kids crammed into the galley with their notebooks, ready to watch their afternoon video for school. Thankfully, the Wrangell Library loaned us several items for long-term use. "Ready," Rayna called out from her perch near the T.V.

"Stanna, can you get it going?" I asked as I rubbed my hands together.

"Sure." She hopped up from her seat and dug out the VHS tape from the pile.

Chapter 15

"Move, you're in my spot." Rob gave Daniel a shove as he hurried past him.

"Boys." I placed my hand on my hip.

This part of the kids' day gave me some quiet time to navigate my thoughts and soul. If only I could shut out the noise of the T.V.

In my room, I pulled out the small radio I'd found in my closet back home as I'd packed. It was in a giveaway pile destined for a second-hand store. I plugged it in, and static blared from the speakers. Was there even a chance of reception out here? Turning the dial, I heard a low, steady voice, and I strained to listen, putting the radio closer to my head.

"Next up is Pastor Leon."

Could it be that I'd happened across a faith-based channel? I carefully turned the knob to fine tune the reception.

"Good afternoon. We will continue our study on spiritual battles. Last week, I spoke of various circumstances we find ourselves in where we can deceitfully feel like we're being lured away." He paused and raised his voice. "But God is always gracious enough to provide a way of escape." I moved my eyes back and forth shocked at what he'd said. This was the very position of my heart.

I pulled out my Bible and the index card. With my pen, I wrote down the verse he cited. Maybe I could steer my heart back to a peaceful course instead of the facade of peace I'd created. I wasn't being fully honest; I was giving my family a false brave face and taking out my own frustrations on them, creating turmoil.

After an hour, the boat's motor went silent, leaving a ringing in my ears. I stood up and hurried to the wheelhouse. What could have stopped us? Did Bill see something that put us in danger? The kids were closing their books and turning off the T.V. as I neared the galley.

"What's going on?" Daniel questioned.

"I don't know." I brushed past him.

Pushing the door open, I went to Bill's side. "What is it?"

"Nothing. Turning it off for a minute. Just look at it. It's beautiful here." He pointed out the window at the tall, craggy mountain face with brilliant-green trees lining the base. He exuded a peace with his focused stare.

Watching his face, I paused to consider that this spectacular view was part of what helped drive him.

"Here." He pointed at the wheel. "Steer us in."

"Uh, no thanks." I pushed back at his outstretched hand.

"Okay, call Rob." He started the engine, avoiding my gaze, and walked out to toss a crab pot and pick up some gear.

The boat rose with a swell in the water, and I held the doorjamb as I searched for Rob. With each step, the motion increased, and I tried to see out of a window while I searched for the help Bill asked for. It wasn't in me. I couldn't help, but I knew we needed someone at the helm.

"Rob," I called out, trying to maintain my balance. The sea had been calm a minute ago.

Stanna came up the stairs from the lower deck that the kids referred to as *the basement*. "He's helping Daniel mark the buoys. Remember, Dad said they could wait until after school?"

"Drat." I turned and struggled to walk straight with the angle of the boat leaning into the wave. Why were we slanted? Gripping the table and then the wall, I eased back to the wheelhouse with my teeth clenched.

The piercing sound of the wind threatened to deafen me as I went in and reached for the black helm to steer. I gripped the column and watched for Bill's signals. He turned to look at me from where he stood with one hand on his hood to keep it from blowing off. His eyes widened when they landed on mine, and he gave me a short smile and pointed to the right. With the power of the wind drilling us from the left, I leaned into the wheel and held it with a widened stance. I looked out at the water where white caps formed. We'd gone from calm waters to at least three- or four-foot seas. How did Bill figure we'd set pots in the storm? Or would this be part of our new normal as well?

Rob and Daniel walked out close to Bill, with the buoys in tow on a line. I watched Bill for more directions, and he motioned for me to hold the position. He and the boys attached the buoys to the first pot, and I saw Daniel slip on the deck and veer close to the other side.

"No!" I shouted out even though they couldn't hear me.

Rob crouched down and reached for Daniel, pulling him up.

They assisted Bill with one last pot and held onto one another coming toward the door.

Why are we doing this?

My forearms burned from holding the wheel in place against the force of the wind. "C'mon, c'mon," I said over the howling. I couldn't steer my thoughts, why did Bill think I could handle the boat?

Bill and the boys came to the wheelhouse and pushed the door closed to keep the spray of water from coming onto the deck. Bill motioned the boys back inside the living quarters and stepped next to me.

"Hold on." His eyes implored me. "I've got to drop the anchor." His wet coat reached past me to the controls.

"Anchor? Why? Why would we stay in this?" I cried out.

"We can ride it out to the end," Bill answered with a calm voice, as he reached for the helm. "I've got to set the rest of the pots before we move out."

I let go, and my heavy arms fell to my sides. Ride it out? How'd he see past the strength of the windstorm?

"Thanks for your help."

After shaking my hands, I wrapped them around my waist. "You're welcome."

He narrowed his eyes. "You okay?"

"Maybe this gets easier?" I blurted out.

"I'm sure it will. We'll learn every step of the way and be able to do more and more." He checked the gauges on the switch panel. "And I don't expect this wind to last long. The barometer is holding, not lowering."

"I'm stunned at all you've learned and how you stay calm. I'm a wreck." I stepped closer to him, wanting to see what he saw in this new life.

"What'd you say this cove is called again?" I asked, not remembering what he'd told me earlier in the day.

"Walker Cove."

"I'd say it's more like Blow-Bad Bay." I pulled my hair back in a ponytail.

Bill laughed and reached for a chart on the console. "I like that, I'm going to pencil it in."

The boat rose and fell in the swelling seas. Could I let the rocking settle me, or would each movement of the waves continuously mock my efforts to captivate a healthy mindset?

CHAPTER 16

THE DAMP COLD OF NOVEMBER CLUNG TO MY FLEECE coat as I sipped tea down in the basement. Our kids had found a Nintendo set at the second-hand store that they could play down there. At times, I would escape to the space for a reprieve, a change of view, hopes of warmth, or an opportunity to read a book.

A stampede of loud steps echoed down the narrow stairs and the kids pushed past each other.

"Hey," I called out. "Slow down." I raised my knees closer to my chest and put my book down.

"Oh, sorry, Mom, we didn't know you were down here," Daniel explained. "We have a competition to finish. Want us to come back?"

His thoughtfulness was endearing. Maybe I should move to a different spot and give them their space. "It's okay, I'll go up."

I walked up the stairs and let out a sigh. Bill was busy outside. I figured Stanna was doing her schoolwork on her bunk. The rest of the kids shouted over the game.

What next? Maybe I should find the knitting I'd started months ago when we'd first come on the boat? I shuffled to my room and dug around in a small tote under our bed. I found a couple of skeins of yarn but no patterns. I let out a long, drawn-out sigh as I sat down in a heap on the bed and fumbled with the yarn between my fingers.

"What are you doing, Mom?" Stanna asked as she peeked her head in my room.

"Nothing. I thought I'd do some knitting, but I can't find a pattern. Are you done with your class?" I patted the bed next to me. She positioned herself with crisscrossed legs on the bed, placing the book in her hand next to her.

"I wanted to show you this part of my science class. I've seen Grandpa do some grafting before but never really understood what he was doing."

A picture of my father-in-law with his fruit trees lined up in the early spring months came to mind. It had been his passion for decades. "Yes, he was very good at that."

"It's kind of neat because it just so happens that my Bible class was talking about grafting too." She leaned forward and opened her booklet, flipping the pages. "There were some personal questions to go along with the devotional, and I thought maybe you could help me."

"Sure." I was flattered she'd included me.

"It says that sometimes we have sinful habits that start in our youth, and we need to seek God's strength to help identify the weak areas. It's taken from, hm, let me see here." She flipped the pages of her book. "James one, verse twenty-one." She looked up at me. "Do you have your Bible handy?"

"Yeah, I'll get that." I reached down beside my bed and opened it up to the verse. I read it silently. "I'm not tracking how this fits with what you said."

"My version says this, 'Wherefore lay apart all filthiness and superfluity of naughtiness, and receive with meekness the engrafted word, which is able to save your souls.' And the question asks, 'Does the word of God cut and pierce? Bind it there until it becomes a part of your character.'" She leaned back on her arms. "I've never thought of the Bible like that. I can see Grandpa working the branches and making them stick."

"I like that image," I replied. "What a neat way to explain it." I placed my bookmark in the page.

"How do you do that in your life?" she asked and watched me for a response.

The prickling truth was that I hadn't made it a habit lately. It had been my goal, but I wasn't letting the scripture cut, pierce, or bind. Instead, it ran over the surface like water off a duck's back. "I'll tell you how I *should* be doing it." I pulled out the index card from the back of my Bible. "I should be memorizing verses more like I used to when I was younger. My friend Amanda and I used to take chunks and memorize them together."

"Cool. Will you do that with me?" Her smile filled her face and lit her kind green eyes.

"Yes. Would you like to memorize the ones I already wrote down before we left Oregon?" I offered.

"Sure. But how do we do the second part?" She tilted her head to the side.

"What do you mean?"

"It says, 'bind it there until it becomes part of your life.'"

I looked down at my Bible and brushed the cover with my hand. "That's a good question. I'm afraid I haven't been doing that well lately."

"Maybe this picture will help you as it did me," Stanna offered, holding out the ribbon from her Bible horizontally. "If the length of this ribbon is the whole event, you don't have to complete it all in one day." She went one finger width down the ribbon. "It's not a sprint, Mom. It's a marathon." She inched her finger toward her Bible one more space. "You serve until the finish line, no quitting, no stepping out of the race."

"And how did you get to be so smart?" I asked her as I reached for her hand.

"Aw, thanks, Mom. I'm gonna write these out now." She jumped up and left the room like she was racing to the finish line.

A chill ran down my back. I went to the kitchen to boil some water. A cup of tea would help warm me from the inside out. While I waited for the water to heat up, I looked around the small space. I opened the cupboard and searched for the brightest mug I could find. With all the gray sky masking the light and adding to the clammy atmosphere on the boat today, I longed to add color to my world.

I poured hot water from the kettle in my mug and, shuddered as I dipped my tea bag in, wrapped my arm around my abdomen. I'd become such a dark rain cloud on the boat. Perhaps it had nothing to do with the skies, rain, or fishing. All that I was doing to make things better was amounting to nothing. I figured I needed warmth, something to do, or time away, but I was running in the wrong direction, kind of like Jonah. I'd been letting myself brush over verses but not letting them stick. My grafting efforts were pretty pathetic.

WE ENTERED A THICK ENGULFING FOG IN THE LATER part of November. With a decrease in temperature and not much warmth to the sun, the moisture in the air hardly burned off during the day. Together, we'd brainstormed about schoolwork we could do as a family, and Bill suggested some books he'd grown up with. We sat shoulder to shoulder in the galley, and I read aloud to the kids while they doodled. As I read to them, my mind wandered, recalling times when I was growing up and how I'd enjoyed the fall with harvest parties, friends, and bonfires. This was going to be a very different holiday season.

"Wait, wait." Rayna cackled. "Can you read that again." She broke out into hysterical laughter.

I'd been so absorbed in my own thoughts I had to search the page to find where I was. "What?" I looked around at everyone as they laughed.

Mr. Poppins Penguins was a hit with everyone. Maybe I'd said something wrong?

"Oh, I can just see the penguins doing that. Making the basement into an ice rink and slides." Rayna curled up and held her stomach. "Can you imagine if we opened all the windows and let water in so the porpoises would be happy in our boat?"

Rob piped up from his corner seat. "Or we kept the basement full of fish for them to eat. You could toss them up, and I'd have them do tricks for their treats." He jumped up and clapped like his hands were flippers. "Ork, ork." Then he hopped around with his feet together.

We laughed at his impersonation. What a clown he was, happy to entertain.

"I haven't seen any porpoises in a while," I stated as I put my finger in the book to hold the spot.

The kids' smiling faces turned serious.

"We saw a whole bunch of them just yesterday," Daniel said. "They were playing in our wake. It was spectacular. I bet there was about ten of them."

Laura stood up and wrapped the blanket that was on her lap around her shoulders. "And a couple of days before that there was a whole bunch of them playing ahead of us like we were chasing them."

I gulped back. Where had I been? I'd missed it all.

"Oh, and then you guys remember the shark we saw trying to lure the baby porpoise away?" Rayna shook her head. "That bad shark. I'm glad that the baby went with the group and was safe."

I repositioned myself on my seat and looked over at Bill, who raised his eyebrows at me.

Was there more I'd overlooked while I wallowed inside?

"Hey, remember how we saw that boat last week, and I visited with the captain? I forgot to tell you about something he said," Bill said and got up to pour himself more coffee. "I remembered when you started talking about the animals playing. He told me about a crab pot he lost last year. He checked with Fish and Game, and no one had turned it in. He chalked it off as a loss. And about six months later, he got a call from someone in Hawaii."

The kids murmured. "What?"

"Yeah, it's crazy. A guy down there saw a whale pulling something behind itself. The whale came close to his boat, like it was trying to show him. The guy used a hook pole to loosen the line, and there was a crab pot on it. He called the number, and it was the captain's lost pot. It'd traveled all the way from Alaska to Hawaii with a migratory whale." Bill smiled and shook his head. "That's so cool."

"Wow," I said. "You'd think the pot would drag the whale down."

"The power of migration, I guess. Race for the finish line no matter the obstacle," Bill explained. "I can relate. Feels like that sometimes, going from one spot to another and setting pots, hoping we can get all that we can."

Within my mind, his statement created a powerful image of Bill working his fishing like an Olympic sport. I'd not thought of it like that before, but there was grit in an athlete who had their sights on a gold medal. Whether it was a migratory compulsion, the competition of sport, or the driving force of providing, Bill was certainly zealous.

What could I say for myself?

CHAPTER 17

IN EARLY DECEMBER, I COULDN'T REMEMBER WHAT day it was when I woke up in the early morning to help Bill steer the boat while he placed the shrimp pots. The dense fog reduced the visibility, but he'd plotted out measurements as best he could ahead of time, and we navigated with our GPS. My feet tingled from standing in one position for an extended period of time, and I tried to wiggle my toes in my rubber boots. Staring outside, watching Bill and Rob toss the shrimp pots, I tried to hold back my yawns.

Bill waved, and I started the motor and moved us forward to the next drop spot. He worked again to throw out each successive set. Spot shrimp were our prize catch—a hot commodity that the Canadian buyers shipped to Japan. I'd noticed fewer boats chattering on the radio lately and figured we must be among the few fishing into the winter. I supposed the rarity of others out fishing drove Bill further and further into the waters, knowing he may have an edge. However, with each mile out into the fog and deep waters, my mind used more courage than I'd managed to stockpile.

The guys motioned for me to cut the engine. The fog lifted enough that I could make out more of the treetops close to an island we skirted. Early that morning, we'd seen some eagles on the shore nearby. The Bible verse came to mind from Isaiah about mounting up with eagles' wings and having strength to meet life's trials. The image was one I couldn't capture until we'd been on the Alaska waters. Now that I'd watched the eagles soaring high, displaying a regal presence, my curiosity was ignited by how God encouraged us to picture the strength He gave like that of the mighty creature.

I started the engine again, and we moved slowly to one more location where, as Bill had explained to me earlier, we'd anchor for a few hours. I'd never have imagined I would be at the helm. Now it seemed like a much simpler chore than throwing pots or rigging them out of the water. After I turned off the engine, I repositioned my ball cap and went into the galley.

"Hi, Mom," Laura said from the table. "I made some fresh coffee."

"Well, thanks." I sat down with a thud and rubbed my eyes to help wipe away the fog of disorientation that nagged me. Without reference to land and sky, it felt like we wandered aimlessly.

"What else can I get you?" Laura asked as she poured a cup of hot coffee into a bright-blue mug that I'd claimed as my own.

I blinked up at her, curious as to why she was doting on me. "I'm good, thanks." I smiled at her and watched as she tidied a few things by the sink. It was good to see her gain confidence in helping with cooking and helping her dad. She had a nice balance in her character of domestic skills as well as with this new maritime career change where she learned along with the rest of the older kids about nautical charts, tides, and marine ecosystems.

I sipped my coffee, looked out the window, and watched the fog slowly rise from the surface of the water, showing a hopeful sign of a brighter day.

Chapter 17

"It looks like it might be a nice day to jig for halibut," Laura offered.

"Don't let it fool you. It's still pretty cool out there." I shuddered. Standing out on the deck in the frigid mist didn't appeal to me. Maybe come summer I'd be up for trolling for some salmon.

Laura sat down across from me. "Yeah, but I didn't have a turn yet. I don't care if it's cold."

I'd forgotten she didn't feel well the day back in October when we'd let the kids out on the deck to try their hand at catching halibut. The bottom dwellers were tasty and fun to reel in. Rob was the first to bring a fifty-pounder to the surface. Now that it was over, I smiled at the thought. These were the memories they'd tuck away and treasure.

Even with the coffee settling in my belly the lure of a nap pulled at me. "Maybe it'll work out," I answered her and stood up to put my mug in the sink. "I'm going to lay down for a bit before we start school." I patted her shoulder as I passed. "Thanks again for the coffee."

I went back to our room and climbed on top of the bed and stared up at the white ceiling.

The fog, the damp, the chill, the newness, the weight of teaching the kids all swirled in my thoughts. I turned over and brushed my hand on Bill's pillow. His determination to be profitable gave him something to focus on, and at night, he shared how much he reveled in mastering his new career. I didn't hold back that I struggled, and Bill always gave me an encouraging word. Why wasn't it enough?

Rolling over, I let the gentle rocking of the boat sooth me.

A sweet smell tickled my nose, reminding me of the aroma of cotton candy at the local county fair. Where was it coming from?

I stretched and looked at my clock. Good land, I must have fallen asleep and napped for three hours. I jumped up and put on my hat that I'd set on the bed. Why hadn't anyone woken me up?

I stumbled into the kitchen where the family sat playing a card game at the table. "I'm sorry, I fell asleep."

Rayna scrambled up from her chair over by the stove and leaned against the counter. "Oh, it's okay. Daddy said to let you sleep."

I moved to sit over by Bill, but he stood up in from of me. He leaned over and gave me a kiss. "Happy Birthday, my amazing Grace." He gave me a hug.

My birthday? I'd forgotten.

"Surprise!" Rayna jumped toward me. She pointed at a lopsided cake set on the stove top. "Daddy made it." Squaring her shoulders back she pointed up at Bill.

"Sorry, babe. You know the whole galley is slanted so your cake has quite the angle to it." Bill pointed at the pan. "But hopefully it tastes the same."

My heart fell to the depths of my core at the realization of how low I'd let myself sink. I hadn't kept track of the days well enough to remember my own birthday. Tears welled up in my eyes, and I smiled at my family, who beamed at me. Their faces showed pride and support. "Aw, thanks so much you guys." I wiped a tear cresting my cheek.

"Happy birthday." Stanna came over, reaching out for a hug.

There was strength in eagle's wings, and today I would claim it as my own. My family was showing me they were there to cheer me on out of the fog and into the bright of day.

THAT AFTERNOON AFTER LUNCH, I AGREED TO A birthday of jigging for halibut. Bill pulled out the long poles from the storage bin and helped the kids put the large hooks on their line. Little Rayna did little to control her enthusiasm for the moment and giggled at the stick her daddy handed her. "This is for hitting the fish when we bring it onto the deck," he said, "Do you think you can handle giving it a smack?"

She jumped up and down holding it with both hands. "I can hit it; I can hit it."

"Oh great." Rob complained. "We'll be here all day if we let *her* do it."

"You were little once," I said to Rob in hopes of encouraging him to show patience. I zipped my coat up closer to my chin and walked nearer to Bill.

The sun shone on the bright deck of the boat, and the glare was startling. We'd not seen such a bright day in weeks. There was even a hint of warmth in the rays. I took a pole from Bill after he set a herring on the hook and let out the line into the water until I felt the weight hit the bottom. "I have to admit, I've never gone fishing for my birthday before." I jigged the line and smiled up at Bill.

"Maybe you'll catch yourself some supper." He rubbed my shoulder.

With my birthday in December, it was usually celebrated with a campfire out in the backyard. Bill had never made me a cake before. He'd always relied on my mom to make my favorite chocolate cake with a creamy mousse filling and rich icing on top. I wasn't much for sweets, but I loved a decadent cake yearly on my birthday. The fact that Bill set aside the time to plan and prepare my dessert sent me a clear message that he was trying to show me his love, not just tell me.

The kids took turns with jigging since we didn't have enough poles for all of them. "Oh, oh," Daniel cried out. "I think I have one."

I widened my stance so I could twist a little and watch him

reel in. He pulled and reeled with Bill standing close by to offer a hand.

"Yup, keep it coming." Bill guided him with his voice.

Daniel's pole curved with tension, and he hung his tongue out like he always did when he concentrated. He tucked it back in his mouth and cheered as the fish crested the water, and he pulled the halibut up into the boat. The halibut fought back, flapping around, and Bill grabbed the line to help steady it so we could gaff it.

Rayna came charging forward with her stick in hand. "Let me at him, Dad."

I could hardly believe my eyes as I watched the kids work as a team to gaff the fish and hold the line for Daniel, who stood proud of his catch.

"How big do you think it is?" Daniel questioned as Bill helped him over to our fish scale.

"You tell me." Bill helped him hook it on, and Daniel reached to see the measurement.

"Thirty pounds. Man, it felt more like seventy." Daniel carried the halibut over to the large bin placed at the stern for our catch.

"It's plenty big and more than enough to cook up for your mom's birthday supper." Bill unhooked the fish and put more bait on the hook. He held up the pole. "Whose turn next?"

I didn't suppose many women could say they'd eaten fresh halibut from the Pacific Ocean on their birthday. This would be one to remember along with the cake made by my husband, who had never baked before.

Bill handed the pole to Stanna and half-jogged inside.

Not sure what he was up to, I continued to dip my pole up and down and watch the surface of the water. Even though we were in water about eighty to ninety feet deep, I kept watching as though I might see a fish close by. I hadn't grown up fishing, so it was all new, and I started to see some of the excitement to what was not only our living, but also a sport.

I felt a tug on my line, and I gave it a yank. The pulling continued, and I began to reel it in. "I've got one," I shouted out, looking over my shoulder to see if Bill was close. The tug-of-war continued as I steadily turned the reel. "You ready with the bonker?" I asked Rayna.

She stood beside me and glared at my line over the water. I smiled at her intensity. She was quite the girl, ready for action.

"Alright, let me bring it in the boat, it's almost to the top. I see it now."

The halibut tried to swim away, but my hook was set. I reeled a little more, then pulled it up into the boat. It smacked the bottom with a force and wiggled. Rayna tried to gaff it, but it was wiggling all over, making quite the scene.

"I'll get it," Rob called out. He must have reeled in his line to help me.

"Go for it." I gripped the pole and watched him take over.

"Here ya go. Not only do you have to cook the dinner, but you have to catch it, too." Rob handed me the end of my line close to where the halibut bit the hook.

I held it up. "It's fish tacos tonight."

Rayna cheered and bounced up and down. "I love tacos."

"Wow, look at you," Bill said from behind me. "Just in time."

I turned to show him my fish and held it up higher. "Oh, yeah? Why you say that?"

"That was the radio. They're calling for a bad storm. We need to move and hunker down." Bill reached for my line. "Here, I can take it for you."

"Thanks." At least there was a bit of fun we could look back on. I rubbed my hands together and gave them a light shake.

"Seriously, everyone. Let's get in and put things away." Bill walked over to where the other halibut sat in some water and brought it back over with him.

The kids scattered inside, and I stood out with Bill on the deck. "Thanks again. That was fun."

Bill's smile was flattened, and he didn't cheer me on like he usually did. "This is a serious storm coming with high winds. Once we're inside, I'm going to need your help to go through the boat and make sure things are secured."

"Okay," I answered and bit at my lip.

Just when I thought I might be able to enjoy myself and keep my head up out of the fog of disbelief and doubt, a storm brewed, threatening to toss us around. Did I have a target on my back?

CHAPTER 18

The older kids helped Bill outside while I worked with Rayna inside to tidy up any loose ends before the storm threatened to overtake us. We'd become pretty lax with leaving bigger items out instead of securing them, but wasn't that part of making it feel like home?

"What about this?" Rayna held out the cake Bill had made earlier.

"Can you find room in a drawer?" I picked up the cards from the table and gathered a few more loose items, putting them in the oversized drawers under our seats at the table.

The familiar howl of a fierce wind began to creep in like a mountain lion stalking its prey. At least we knew who and where the enemy was.

"Oh, I don't like that sound." Rayna plopped herself down on a seat. "It means all the fun is over."

"I'm sorry. You'll need to lie on your bed until the worst is over." I wished they could watch another video from the library, but it would be near impossible while being tossed about.

"Yeah, but I'd rather be fishing or helping Daddy outside." She crossed her arms across her chest.

I appreciated that she was my outdoor girl, but I knew there were few ways to entertain while laying down on their bunks.

Everyone else came in, and we scattered to pick up items in their rooms. Bill explained what needed to be done, and I gladly went to our room to do my part. After I secured our things, I laid down on the bed and closed my eyes.

So much for cruising the waters and coasting along. From one place to the next, we'd formed a pattern of setting pots and returning to retrieve our catch within a day or two. Would waiting out the storm set us back with Bill's schedule? He'd promised we'd be done soon and dock in Wrangell for a break.

"Grace?" Bill called out.

I stood up and felt the boat moving. If Bill was calling, who was driving?

"Yes," I answered him before I could see him and hurried to the wheelhouse where I found him and Rob.

"It's the anchor," he said in a serious voice. "I loosed it, but it's not up all the way in the chain locker. I need you to help Rob steer while I try and see what's going on." He placed his hand on my shoulder.

"Okay." It was all I knew to answer, but I was clueless as to how I was going to help. The waves were rising, and the boat was already taking a beating from the wind. I knew the importance of having the anchor in the locker ready to release when we were at our stopping point. Any more fudging with it, and we could be tossed with the waves and not able to secure ourselves safely.

Dear Lord, Keep Bill safe out there.

Bill walked out, bracing himself on the gear, and then I lost sight of him.

The boat moved with the water, and I held the wheel

straight. "Do we just try and keep it faced into the wind?" I asked Rob, hoping he knew the answer.

"Your guess is as good as mine. Dad said for me to watch the control panel and see if the anchor loosens and when it does, to try reeling it in again." Rob kept his gaze on the controls.

Hold the post, hold firm. I instructed to myself. *Face it head-on. Face it, face it.*

As I gripped the wheel, my palms started to sweat and I watched the deck for any sign of Bill. "How's it look now?" I asked even though it had only been seconds since we spoke.

"Nothing different."

I heard the tension in his voice. My heart raced, and I concentrated on taking in a deep breath. How long should we do this before we worry for Bill? What if he'd slipped and was hurt, or worse, he was overboard?

A larger wave rose in front of us, and I strengthened my hold and braced my feet. *Face it, Grace.* The boat rose with a heave, and I leaned forward to brace myself. Coming back down, I pictured Bill out on the bow, clinging to it for dear life.

"It's going." Rob shouted out and clicked the switch. The sound of the gears of the anchor moving was sweet music to my ears. We just needed to see Bill to know the worst was over. Certainly, now we could hurry to the cove where we needed to shelter.

C'mon Bill. C'mon. I didn't know if I should start the motor or continue to let the boat ride the waves. It seemed like we were sitting ducks.

"Want me to go look for him?" Rob offered.

I flashed my eyes at him. "No." There was no way I was going to let one more person out in the storm.

Straining to see out the window as the wind whipped up the water, I breathed a prayer out loud. "God, hurry."

Bill's bright orange rainslicker came into view, and I let out the breath I'd been holding. He moved with careful, slow steps, steadying himself.

"Thank you, Lord." I watched Bill's face, anticipating the look of reassurance he always gave me. His gaze met mine, and I saw a look of worry in his blue eyes.

He opened the door and shook the water from his coat before hanging it up on a hook. Without a word, he reached for the wheel, and I stepped back. Turning on the power and starting the engine, he spoke over the noise of the wind. "Thanks."

"What now?" Rob asked the question that was in the forefront of my thoughts.

"We're headed for shelter from the wind." Bill looked straight ahead without lifting his eyes.

"What was wrong with the anchor?" Rob queried as he braced himself on a nearby ledge.

"Not sure. Will have to look at it later." Bill's short answer made me wonder if there was a bigger problem that he wasn't telling us about. Was there more danger to skirt?

"Is it okay if I head back?" I needed to go find something that would help me find the security I longed for so I could imagine that we were simply in our home away from home and coasting to a safe haven.

"Yup, I've got this." Bill replied as he gave me an abrupt flattened smile of worry.

I walked away certain there were more ends that were not just loosened but possibly frayed and unraveling.

MOST OF OUR TRIP WAS IN THE DARK, AND MY SENSES were on high alert as I listened to the howl of the wind. By the light of a headlamp, I sat on Rayna's bunk and read aloud to the kids on their bunks, hoping to give them a sense of security and, in a way, shelter them from the reality of the storm outside. I went back and forth between them to Bill, checking if he needed anything. Each time I approached him, I asked with apprehension if everything was okay. His quick "yup" each time brought me little peace.

After going to ask for Bill's assurance one last time, I walked back to check on the kids, then went to the galley so I'd be closest to Bill. Why didn't he share his fears with me? We were a team.

I tried to steady myself while I retrieved a magazine from the drawer under the seats. Holding the book in my hand, I leaned my head back and closed my eyes.

Bill and I *had been* a team before the cougar attack, and that had been the kickstart of our new life. This adventure was changing us. Was it for the better?

If the cougar had never attacked, where would our family be?

There had to be a part of this that made us all better. If not, then what was the point? I grabbed the table and stood up. I yearned to know what fear furrowed in Bill's strained brow. If it wasn't something certain, what did he sense?

He didn't hear me enter the wheelhouse. I reached for his shoulders and gave them a massage, then leaned over and whispered in his ear. "I've got you. How's it going?"

I felt his shoulder drop beneath my hands, and I hoped he was finding some relaxation from my touch.

"We're almost there," he stated.

"Okay, good." The promise of peaceful waters certainly lessened the strain in his voice, but I wanted to know for sure. "I know I've skirted wanting to be a part of this, but is there something wrong?" I let the question out.

"Oh, nothing much. Just ready to turn in and get some rest." He pointed ahead to a rocky alcove. "We'll sneak in just past there. Then it's time for birthday cake." He turned to look at me and gave me a brief smile.

"Right." I had forgotten about the displaced party that we'd tucked aside.

Bill put his arm around me. "I guess this will be a birthday to remember, huh?"

"That's for sure." I tried to brace myself against the wave ahead of us.

Bill turned the boat and increased speed to hurry into the circle of safety. As soon as we skirted the rock, I could see the flat waters ahead of us and the promise of rest. I watched Bill as he eased off the throttle and let the boat coast in so we didn't create much of a wake. He checked the depth of the water, switched off the power, and pushed the settings for the anchor to drop. The control rattled.

"What?" he asked out loud. He flipped the switch off, then back on again, and it knocked some more. Turning it off he let out a deep sigh. "Hold the wheel. I'll be back."

"Alright." I reached for the control. Why did I avoid helping this way? All I needed to do was follow Bill's lead. It didn't mean conforming to his dream—just being a part of it. I stood a little taller and thought of the cake he'd made. He'd never done anything like that before. He was changing himself for me. Certainly, I could do the same for him.

Bill wasn't gone more than a couple of minutes. "Not sure what the deal is, but hopefully it'll work now." He let the anchor out and sighed as it landed on the ocean floor. "Oh, thank God. Now we can rest tonight and head out in the morning to retrieve our pots."

"Really? So soon?" When would we slow down our pace?

"Yup, first thing in the morning." He turned off the engine and wiped his wet hands on his pants. "Now let's go find that cake."

"Sure." I agreed and hoped that the following day Bill might consider camping in place a little longer. "Is everything okay with the boat? Anything more I can help with?" I rubbed my hands together to warm them from the chill in the air.

Bill furrowed his brow. "I think we're good." He looked at me from of the corner of his eye.

Were there things hanging over his head that he'd brushed aside because I wasn't much help? I shrugged and followed him back to the galley to take the cake out of the drawer and celebrate the evening of my birthday in the calm waters of the bay.

CHAPTER 19

THE NEXT MORNING, I WOKE UP TO THE BONE-chilling sound of something scraping the sides of the boat. My heart pounding, I jumped up and ran to the wheelhouse in my pajamas. "Bill," I called out before I saw him.

What was going on? My stomach churned at the thought of rock cutting at the metal bottom.

Flashing a glance outside, the sheen on the water was oddly dull. Were we stuck in something?

Bill sat at the helm with his back to me, and I hurried to his side. "What is it?" I asked, catching my breath.

His face was intent on the waters beside us. "There's fresh water on the surface. We're breaking through."

"Breaking?" The crackling sound like clinking glass sent a chill down my back. "Why are you so calm? This can't be good." I searched Bill's eyes for help.

"It's okay." He turned to me. "Sounds much worse than it really is."

"You've got to be kidding me. If we take on ice, we could start to sink." My core quivered, and I closed my eyes in an attempt to stay calm. "How do you know?" I attacked his reasoning.

"There's not enough ice to—"

I cut him off. "Like you know. We've never done this before."

His silence didn't answer my accusations, nor did it calm my racing heartbeat. He flattened his lips and looked out the window.

I swallowed to help moisten my dry throat and clenched my teeth. Where could I escape the image of us sinking to the bottom of this bay?

"I know enough," Bill whispered. "And we're headed to get our pots. Get the kids up and focus on doing some school."

Turning on my heels, I moved from him and went straight for our room where I fell onto the bed with my hands over my ears. *Oh, Lord, help me. I can't stand it.* The chills and tingling ran down my legs like the sting of a jellyfish.

Could I control how my body responded to the noise?

"Oh, God, help me." I trembled in prayer.

Be still, and know that I am God. The verse from Psalms burst into my thoughts like a lightning bolt.

"More, God, more." Would He continue to pull me up?

My grace is sufficient. His reminder brought breath to my lungs. And I removed my hands from my ears.

All scripture is given by inspiration of God, and is profitable for doctrine, for reproof, for correction, for instruction in righteousness: That the man of God may be perfect, thoroughly furnished unto all good works.

The last verse was the one Amanda had suggested I memorize. Stanna and I had done just that. It had been a series of rote words that had sunk in but hadn't resounded. I saw it now; God was giving me what I needed. He was enabling me to lean on Him. With His word.

"Oh, God, I need You!" I lifted my hands to Him and closed my eyes. "Promise me more." I pushed out the words as an offering.

Finally, my brethren, be strong in the Lord, and in the power of His might.

"Yes, thank You, Lord." Another verse of truth that He would empower me with His strength. Leaning over, I fell on my face, humble before my God and King. Why hadn't I called out to Him like this before?

"God, You know I cannot serve You in my own strength. I need the Holy Spirit's help. I'm giving You my life to direct because on my own I'm a stressful mess." The warm tears fell off my cheeks and onto my bed. I wiped most that remained from my face, but one salty tear rolled into my mouth. The briny taste was like the ocean, reminding me I was at war on a boat and the enemy was dragging me down.

Get up. Trust Me to see it through; to equip you.

I didn't audibly hear Him, but the prompt from God was clear. After wiping my face with my hands, I grabbed a tissue and blew my nose. "Yes, Lord," I answered and changed my clothes. Not only was I putting on a fresh set of clothes, I was also clothing my heart and mind with the truth. I wanted to cling to Him. I longed to not just walk but leap into His arms and become more like Him.

THE HAZE, MISTY RAIN AND CLOUD COVER FELT LIKE an umbrella of protection after the harsh winds of the previous day and icy breakwaters of earlier. I'd nestled in the galley with a blanket over my lap and my Bible on the table. Fresh coffee perked on the stove top, and for the first time ever, I sensed the familiar feeling of home.

After breakfast, the kids hurried through their schoolwork and decided to play a game in the basement.

Bill hadn't made his way in yet. Perhaps I'd pushed too hard? Over the years, we'd understood the depth of the description *one flesh*. He completed me in more ways than I truly understood. However, the inciting incident with the panther was like a spark that set a ring of fire between us. The circus show wasn't entertaining anymore. The distance was widening, and I wanted to bridge the gap.

I opened my Bible to the verses I'd highlighted as a young wife, and I smiled at the memory of our early years. We'd made promises to one another at various steps along the way. Some regarding us as a couple and others involving the kids. Why hadn't I clung to the Word like I'd promised? How could I help mend this pattern?

Bowing my head, I whispered, "God, help me bring peace to my marriage and family. Help me to draw on your greatest riches given to me because of Christ Jesus."

Finishing my prayer, I opened my eyes and saw Bill standing in the doorway to the galley. He must have paused when he heard me praying. Now he moved to the stove top and poured a cup of coffee into his oversized thermos.

I tucked the blanket beside me and stood up. "I'm sorry for doubting you earlier." The guilt had been knotted in my stomach all morning

"I forgive you." He spoke with his back to me. "I'm headed back out. Call me for lunch."

As I watched Bill walk back out, the knot twisted in me and threatened to double me over.

CHAPTER 20

IN THE THIRD WEEK OF DECEMBER, WE VENTURED closer to Wrangell. With each nautical mile, I anticipated the feeling of freedom we'd have when we could walk on land again. I imagined myself exploring downtown, looking in the few shops of the city on Front Street, and treating the kids to ice cream at Jerry's. Simple plans formed that presented themselves as luxurious.

I sealed the package of halibut and marked it with a sharpie before I placed it in the freezer. When we arrived in Wrangell, we would send some fish back to family in Oregon. *Huh, my mom will flip when she unpacks this.* She'd mentioned more than once how much she missed fresh seafood.

"Mom?" Stanna called out before she hurried into the galley. "Can I get a new swimsuit when we get to Wrangell? Dad said we can go swimming at the pool."

"Sure." I smiled at her and watched her beam at my answer.

"Thanks."

She'd missed swimming at the city indoor pool so much since we'd left, and she talked about it often. I'd had a sense of guilt that I'd taken it from her when we came on the boat, surrounded by water with nowhere to swim. The icy waters of

Chapter 20

the North Pacific that bordered the Arctic were deadly this time of year, especially away from the beach.

"I hear they have a polar plunge on Wrangell this time of year. Interested?" I asked as I tucked the ziplock bags back in the drawer.

"Uh, no thanks." Stanna walked back out, and I heard her calling out to Rayna about the library books.

The excitement of the day was invigorating. Soon we could stockpile fresh groceries, new books from the library, and maybe go to church while we were there for a few days.

Huh, I might even meet some friends. I pondered the idea of forming friendships on land that could help encourage me while I was away. Maybe it was a silly notion, but wouldn't someone from there understand my trials better than friends back home?

I rinsed off my knife and wiped off the counter. Soon, we'd have an island vacation.

"Half an hour," Bill called out from the doorway.

"Okay," I answered and put the bags of fish in a large bin for hauling off the boat. I turned to ask him a question, but he was already back out the door. He'd been tied to the wheelhouse for the last couple of weeks, saying there were things to watch more closely. I hoped there wasn't more to his absence. The icicles between us were difficult to miss. Perhaps this reprieve would bring us time alone to work out escalating tension.

I hummed a tune I'd heard on the radio earlier that day and organized the to-go pile I'd gathered in the galley.

Rayna came running in with Daniel scrambling behind her.

"Ha, you missed," she yelled out.

"No running inside, you two. We're almost there," I corrected them as I picked up one of the totes and set it on a bench. I was thankful life in this part of Alaska wasn't arctic and there was only a dusting of snow near the beach. We'd be able to spend time outside on solid ground.

"I can't wait to run down the sidewalk all the way into town," Daniel said rapidly.

"Can we go to the park first?" Rayna begged. "I want to go on the monkey bars." She pulled up her sleeve and gripped her biceps. "I think I'm stronger now."

Daniel and I laughed at her strutting.

I envisioned myself out for morning walks on the long bike path that wound along the coast from the city of Wrangell out to Shoemaker Bay. A glorious five-mile walk sounded like an invitation to walk on the moon. Maybe Bill would agree to stay through Christmas with family and perhaps even New Year's. Certainly, we could afford time on land and make the most of it.

Rob and Daniel moved bags of garbage out to the deck while the girls gathered up all our bags.

I stole a look outside. The island of Wrangell greeted us. My eyes followed the hillside up to a small knoll called Mount Dewey. Our nieces and nephews had told us about it and how they loved racing up the boardwalk staircase to the top. One more thing to hope to do on our visit.

The boat slowed down as we entered the harbor, and I let down my stiff shoulders. All the fearful emotions and worry fell off me, and I breathed in the crisp air promising rejuvenation and relaxation. I walked out onto the deck to savor the homecoming.

I scanned the dock. Bill's brother Steve and his family gathered near our slip, waiting to welcome us back. Certainly, the promise of time with his brother would be enough to lure Bill to settle in.

Waving at the family, I smiled and prayed, *God will you use this time to heal our broken pieces and bring peace that passes all understanding?*

Bill called for the boys to let out the buoys that went along the outside of the boat, and we coasted into our slip on the south side of the harbor. Our approach was smooth, and with the engine shutting off, I felt silly about all the expectant thoughts running through my mind. Skip down the street, go grocery shopping, wander the stores aimlessly, and sip coffee at a restaurant that didn't bob up and down with the tossing ocean.

"Hey," I called out to Steve and Kim as I handed each of the kids each an item to carry off the vessel and down to the dock.

I hugged Kim as Bill and Steve shook hands and the kids gave each other high fives, their excited voices filling the harbor.

"Good to see ya. We brought your truck yesterday." Steve reached for a bag to carry. "Here, let me throw those in a cart."

"Thanks." Bill pulled some items off the deck.

"How long will you be here? Have time to stay for some of my famous apple pie at Christmas?" Kim questioned as Steve and Bill worked to fill the cart.

"Nope. Got to get back out." Bill threw a duffle into another cart that Rob had wheeled over. "There's an opener Christmas Day. This will be a turn-and-burn trip."

Turn and burn? He'd already done that. Weren't we working enough? Wasn't there time to at least enjoy the family we did have close by?

"Sorry," I whispered to Kim, wrapping my coat around myself, then pulling my hat down on my head.

What was the reason for chasing each opener when everyone else was docking?

Would Bill hear me if I asked why we couldn't have some freedom from the boat?

AT THE CITY SWIMMING POOL, I SAT WATCHING THE kids climb the inflatable dinosaur in the shallow end. The simple joy of scrambling to the top and falling into the water brought laughter from all of them. Stanna volunteered to watch Rayna so I could sit behind the glass in the comfort of a chair.

I crossed my legs and pulled out my knitting. After one day in town, we'd managed to strike several items off our to-do list. Bill mentioned finishing the grocery shopping and loading back up within twenty-four hours. Thankfully, the kids' begging for time to swim hit a soft spot, and Bill agreed to an evening swim while he worked on some boat repairs.

He hadn't shared the problems with me, and I hadn't volunteered to help. My assumption was that Steve would provide more assistance than I could ever offer.

The constant tug-of-war I felt gnawed at me. I was torn by my desires to help Bill and satisfy the kids' and my own wants.

"Hi." Someone spoke beside me, and I turned to see a young woman with long brown hair. Her smile radiated from her deep brown eyes, which were so cheery that I felt like I already knew her. She flipped her hair to her back.

I returned her greeting and watched her scoot her small children toward the changing room.

"I'm Annie. I don't know that I've met you before." She set down her duffle bag on the bench.

"I'm Grace. We're new and have been out fishing," I explained. I watched Annie's eyes glisten at the mention of fishing.

"My dad loves to fish. Some of my best memories are of spending time with him out on the ocean." She waved at some of the kids in the pool. "Are you moving here, then?"

Her question pricked my ears. Were we? I tossed the idea around like a beach ball on a windy day. Where would it land? "Well, we've committed to fish one year, and we'll see where the Lord takes us after that."

She placed her palm on my shoulder. "You're a Christian?"

Her faith shone at the mention of the term, and I knew that she served the same Lord I did.

"Yes, I am," I said and sat up a little straighter.

"It is so good to meet you. Tomorrow they're having a kids' program at our church while the adults watch a Bible study series on Jonah. Do you think you'd like to join us?" Annie took her coat off and dug through her bag, then pulled out a piece of paper and a pen. "Here I'll write down the time and directions to find the church."

She explained the purpose of the study and how much she'd been learning.

"Mom, are you coming?" A little brown-haired girl poked her head from around the corner, waving at her.

"I better go." Annie picked up her bag. "It'd be great to see you."

As I tucked the paper she'd handed me into my purse, I said, "Thanks for the invite."

Annie popped around the corner again. "I almost forgot. If for some reason you aren't here, we're airing the service over the radio. There's lots of fishing families here that want to be a part of the service and can't. Here, I'll write down the station and the time it will be rebroadcasted."

Thank God for Christian radio.

We waved goodbye again, and I turned my attention to the pool, searching for each of the kids. I imagined walking into a church after all these months away. It was like the welcoming fragrance of a fresh rose growing next to the house. The aroma of another believer who permeated the love of God. I'd missed it so much. Church wasn't a building—it was a body of believers who knew Jesus as their Savior. A family.

"Hey." Bill nudged my shoulder and sat beside me.

"I didn't even hear you come in." I watched his face as he looked through the glass, watching the kids. He smiled and waved at the boys jumping off the inflatable.

"How much longer will they be swimming?"

I checked my watch. "They have another hour."

"Oh." Bill stood up and stretched.

"Did you fix what you wanted?" I questioned, hoping he still needed a few more days.

"Yup, sure did. We can load up with groceries and be off before lunch tomorrow."

I stared up at him. "Really?" There had to be more time. Our visit was beginning to satisfy my need to see other people and explore. We needed more time.

"We've got that opener to get to. We're better prepared for the longer distance now that I know the boat checks out." Bill stood with his hands in his pockets.

"I figured we'd stay longer." I pushed out the words, hoping he'd hear my plea.

"This is our livelihood now. We've got to get back and fish while we can. Remember all those months of nothing?" His eyes searched mine, then he looked away.

"Okay, I'll make my list for the store."

The tug-of-war was over, and I was in the mud.

I'd follow him back to the boat, scramble back into fishing mode, and cheer him on.

CHAPTER 21

IN PREVIOUS YEARS, OUR CHRISTMAS EVE TRADITION included time with our extended family in Oregon. Bill's sister owned a ranch, and after our late afternoon meal, we'd load up in a wagon to go on a hayride. Kids piled into the back, and we sang songs. The jingling of the bells on the horses was like a lullaby that soothed the soul. Afterward, around a large bonfire, we sipped hot cider and ate the gingerbread cookies the kids decorated. Then we gathered under the string of lights hanging in the old barn and played games late into the evening. It had always been that way, until now.

The ringing I heard in my ears was from the noise of the engine as we pushed hard to get out to deep waters before nightfall. Once we were loaded onto the boat, Bill occupied himself in the steering house.

"Mom?" Stanna stood next to me in the galley while we peeled some potatoes for the night's meal. I'd insisted on real potatoes instead of instant.

"Yeah." I scrubbed at the peel and handed it to her.

"Where will you have the stockings tonight? I have a few things to put in for everyone."

"Do you have a suggestion?" I looked around the small space and questioned where we could secure them.

"How about we hide them?" She offered with a giggle. "We can make it a new tradition. I can think of a few good hiding spots."

"I like that." I nudged her with my elbow. "You're good at making lemonade from lemons. At first, thought I was sad we didn't have our mantle to put them on, and here you go, finding a way to liven things up."

"Do you think we can decorate those cookies tonight?"

The packaged gingersnaps and a small tub of icing were far from the usual homemade ones, but they were better than nothing. "For sure. I always love to see what you come up with. You're so creative."

"I have a good teacher." Stanna placed the potato in the pot.

"Mom, Mom." Rayna ran into the galley with a box in her hand. "Where is the Christmas tree?"

Stanna and I both laughed.

"There isn't one." I wiped my hands on a towel. "Do you think it would just pop up out of nowhere?"

"What? No tree? How will we have Christmas?" Rayna threw her hands in the air. "Where will I find my presents?"

I'd bought a few small things for the kids, but Christmas would still be meager compared to other years. "We'll figure out something."

"I'm going to go ask Dad if we can go to an island and get one." Rayna stomped off in pursuit of her daddy.

We'd have to set aside a few of the traditions and focus on the depth and meaning of the day.

I turned on the radio, and Stanna and I sang along with Christmas music while we wrapped the potatoes in foil and seared the meat before placing it in the small oven. Next, we made a cherry salad from whipped topping, sweetened condensed milk, and cherry pie filling. It was more like a dessert, but a favorite dish from Bill's family.

"Would you like me to thaw the rolls now?" Stanna asked as she pulled the rolls out of the small freezer.

"Sure." I reached for some butter that I'd placed in there earlier.

"This is going to be a great meal."

I smiled and sat down on the chair to finish the tea I'd made earlier while doing my devotions.

We could hear Rayna crying before we saw her, and I knew it meant no tree. She walked in, came to sit next to me, and laid her head against me. Her little body shook. Pulling her in close, I rubbed her head. "I'm sorry."

"Do you want to help me find the stockings and put the fudge in them?" Stanna offered to Rayna.

"O-o-okay." Rayna followed her big sister out and wiped her tears from her eyes.

My heart broke for her. What could I muster up to help soften the blow that Christmas would be different and wasn't going to look, feel, or be the same?

I CALLED FOR THE BOYS AND LAURA, AND THEY WAITED for me in the galley.

"Here's the list of what we need to make ourselves a Christmas tree." I handed it to Rob, and he raised his eyebrows as he scanned the list.

"This is going to be interesting," he stated, "and really cool."

"Hurry before Rayna sees you. I'd like to surprise her. I'll find Stanna and have her keep them busy downstairs." Ideas kept rushing at me, and I needed to take action to have the plan in place.

Gathering up paper cups, a skein of yarn, and crayons, I hurried to the basement. "Stanna, I have a project for you," I called out to the girls and found them reading a book together.

"Would you girls like to make me some decorations for the galley? You can make some bells like the ones we used to have back home on the horses." I set the supplies on a T.V. tray.

"Bells?" Rayna walked over and inspected the cups.

"I'll help you." Stanna moved closer to her sister.

"Thanks, girls." I motioned behind Rayna's back at Stanna. I pointed at my watch and held up my hands, signaling ten minutes. She nodded in return.

Upstairs, I explained my plan to Rob, Daniel, and Laura. "Okay, see if you can make a tree with these." I pointed to the fishing poles, ore, and rope.

"Ah, I get it." Laura reached for the ore and held it up. "This is the tree trunk?"

Daniel picked up a fishing pole and slanted it next to the ore. "I'm guessing this is a branch?"

"I do have the smartest kids." I placed my hands on my hips and smiled at them.

After turning up the music, I sang along as I pulled more food out of the fridge for supper and the kids built their tree.

"I hope this counts for school," Rob said. "Isn't this art or something?"

"Sure," I called out over the music. We were all learning so much. How to improvise and make the most of our time. How to make sacrifices for one another.

Bill walked into the kitchen and put his mug in the sink. "What's going on here?"

"We're making a tree." Daniel used some rope to tie the poles to the ore.

"Hun, that's pretty neat. Just make sure you put the reels in a safe spot and remember which pole they came off of." Bill leaned against the wall and rubbed his temples before walking back out.

These long days of work were taking a physical toll on him. I saw the dark circles under his eyes. Could I draw him out of it and find a way to press the pause button?

Rob opened a cupboard door and dug through, pulling cans of food out. "Do you have any popcorn in here? I wonder if we can string some to put on the tree since we don't have decorations."

"That's a great idea. But if you can, wait until after we eat." I stood up and checked on the rolls that Stanna had taken out to thaw. "Finish the tree so we can surprise Rayna."

My soul was in tune with the tension Bill had brought into the room. How could we pull off a Merry Christmas?

I walked to the steering house to say something that I hoped I wouldn't regret.

Bill sat at the helm with a chart stretched across his lap.

"Hey." I strolled over to look over his shoulder. "Where's the next drop spot?" Searching the map, I looked for a familiar name I might recognize.

"It's not on this one." He began to fold it up and set it on a nearby ledge.

"Oh." I inched away and looked out the window at the dark waters and black sky. *Lord, give me the words. This season is about You, and I want us to pause and linger over the wonder of it all and celebrate, Immanuel. God with us.*

"We've got to stop. Please. I appreciate that you're determined to fish for every shrimp you can and that that means providing for your family. But today is Christmas Eve." I placed my arm around his shoulder.

"After we drop the pots tonight, we can—"

I didn't let him finish. "Please? Can we stop and come back to that tomorrow?"

Bill hung his head and rubbed his temple. "I'm sorry. I should have let us stay in Wrangell longer." He turned off the motor and checked the GPS. "Okay, we'll stop."

I could count on one hand the times I'd doubted Bill's heart once it was set in motion. But this was one I'd needed to address in hope of helping our whole family. "Thanks," I whispered.

"I'll be there in about a half hour." Bill gathered a few supplies.

I walked out and went to go find Rayna. She'd have a tree. It might be the craziest-looking Christmas tree ever, but she'd have one.

CHAPTER 22

WE GATHERED IN THE BASEMENT AFTER SUPPER TO read the Christmas story from the Bible. We'd always worked to impress on our growing family the depth of the meaning of Christmas: celebrating that Christ came as a baby so He could sacrifice Himself for our sins and bring us peace with God.

After reading from Matthew, we decided to play a game, and the kids' laughter was like the warmth from a fireplace. Normally, our work outside was hard and cold, and this time together felt more like our life back in our log home at the end of a day.

Rayna flicked her last UNO card on the floor and did a jig as she sat crisscrossed. "I won again," she announced.

"Whoo-hoo, the big winner at a little card game," Rob jeered. "How about we play something different?" He reached behind him for a strategic game he'd borrowed from his cousins.

"I think I'm going to take a break from playing." Stanna moved up onto the chair from the floor. "Maybe we could watch a movie?"

Nestled in next to Bill on the floor with some cushions, I smiled at everyone. If all the Christmases before were about family time, we were still succeeding with our makeshift celebration. "Oh, I almost forgot. A lady in Wrangell told me about a special event at their church, and it's going to be rebroadcasted this evening. Let's tune in even if it's for a little bit. It can be like we're at a church candlelight service." I sat up a little straighter and tucked the soft pillow into the small of my back.

Daniel turned the stereo on and tuned it to the correct frequency noted on the paper. Annie had explained that the service was geared toward families, so I was hopeful there would be something for everyone. An upbeat song came on, and we heard kids shouting out the words in the background. I smiled at the image of all the excited kids doing hand motions.

Someone on the broadcast popped on. "Hey everyone, our youth pastor is going to give a short message on the object lessons we find in Jonah."

Our girls laid down on the rug in the middle of the room and played with each other's hair while Daniel and Rob found their sketch books.

"Is there someone in your life who has mistreated you?"

Immediately, I thought of the youth worker who'd lied to me and my friends and left me resentful.

"Perhaps you've thought, like Jonah did, that they had it coming, and you wished they'd get their punishment."

Certainly, that was how I'd felt all these years.

"God's heart is for all to be saved. Anyone here glad that God was patient with them?"

Cheers in the background erupted, and I nodded. Yes, God was gracious with me.

Rayna stood up and flicked at the braids Stanna had tied off for her. She went over to pick up a coloring book and sat next to me. I rubbed her back and watched her pick out some crayons from a box.

"Jonah was rebuked for his attitude toward the Ninevites,

Chapter 22

and then Jonah made a request from God. He wanted to resign from his work. Have you ever been tired of the work your parents asked you to do?" The youth pastor questioned.

"Um-hm, every day," Rayna said.

Bill shook his head, and I raised my eyebrows at him. I'd been guilty of this attitude from the moment we'd stepped on the boat. I'd found multiple ways to zone out and obsess with things in hopes of distracting myself. But those things only left me empty and angry.

The speaker pushed it to the next level. "God knows where your heart is: in your obedience. Maybe you're saying, 'Yes, Mom,' but inside, you're grumbling."

Rayna's eyes widened as she looked up at me. Little did she know I felt the same guilt.

"I'll challenge all of you to be thankful for what's in front of you. God allows these difficulties so you will be ready to do something different."

I gulped back. These months were challenging me to the core.

"Jonah was angry. He wanted God to justify his attitude and be on his side." I could hear the speaker shuffle some papers. "Stand up if you've ever played a game where teams were picked. Go ahead, jump up. There you go."

I could hear the rumble of murmurs in the crowd and imagined kids happy to get up off the floor and get their wiggles out.

"Now, go ahead and answer in your head if you've ever grumbled because you didn't get picked for the team you wanted to be on. I know, I'm there with you. I have. And you know what? I've pouted about it too. See my pouty face."

Giggles spread, and our kids laughed.

"I can picture it." Laura said, raising her hand.

"Guess what?" the speaker continued. "God doesn't yield to our pouting. Nope, not for a second. Let's stand together and say that we will choose to want what God wants. I'll say it again. What God wants. What God wants. It might be hard. It might be really hard. But with God's help, you can do it without pouting and with a happy heart. Let's raise our voices in praise with a song to our good God."

The rustle of the rest of the crowd standing up muffled the speaker and the group started singing a familiar song our family had sung in church back in Oregon.

"Hey, I know this one," Daniel said, and he stood up.

I looked around, and we all rose to our feet in the small space. Bill put his arm around me. I put my arm around Rayna, and we all formed a circle, hugging and singing together. God had put the reminder in my heart to listen to the program, and it was what I needed to hear. The truths I'd known for years, that I'd taught to my kids and had worked to apply myself.

After our worship time, we played a game, and then I went upstairs to pull out supplies for decorating cookies. Laura followed me up.

"Go ahead and pull out the icing along with the plastic spoons," I said. I placed the cookie tin on the counter and set the kettle on the stove to boil water for cider.

"This is just like Christmas Eve back home," Laura said as she put the sprinkles on the table. "Cider, cookies, and instead of a hay ride, it's a boat ride." She giggled.

Bill came up and pulled out the coffee from the canister.

"Planning an all-nighter?" I questioned as I rubbed against his shoulder.

His quizzical face with wrinkled eyebrows and half-smile told me he most certainly was. "The work never stops. Never."

Unsure of why I'd imagined it to come to an abrupt halt, I smiled back at him and patted his arm. "Need me to drink a cup too?"

Bill smiled. "I'm headed out to move us into the cove a little further and to set anchor."

Chapter 22

"Okay." I pulled the cider packets out of the container and set them on the table, then looked out the window to try and see where we were. I'd been so engrossed with Christmas Eve that I hadn't noted any landmarks.

"Oh, Mom. I love my tree so much," Rayna said as she walked in. "Can we take a picture of it?"

"Can you ask Stanna? I think she has the camera." I turned off the kettle. "And tell the boys it's time to decorate cookies."

I grabbed my coat from the hook and went out to touch base with Bill about the presents I'd picked up for the kids. In the steering house, Bill was taking notes. The cool air of the evening tickled my nose. This would be the coldest Christmas of my life, with humidity and temperatures near zero. "I didn't pay much attention to where we were going today. What's tonight's anchor spot?" I peeked out the window into the dark of night and could see the silhouette of a mountain covered in the shining moonlight of a clear night. I'd come to learn that clear meant the cold from a high barometric pressure.

"We'll sneak a little further into Walker Cove for a few hours, then I'll pull anchor and head out." He folded his notebook closed and searched my face. "Thanks for making this a great Christmas Eve."

"Awe, you're welcome." I ran my hand through my hair. "Do you have those gifts for the kids in here?" We'd given each of the kids twenty dollars to shop in Wrangell for the family gift exchange. Bill and I also picked up small pocketknives for everyone.

"Yup, I can bring them in." He stood up and wrapped his arms around me. His coat was chilly against my skin, but I also felt the warmth of his affection.

"Wait." I pulled away from him. "Walker Cove? Isn't that where we were iced in?" The realization hit me like a chunk of glacier falling into the ocean and creating a wave.

"We have no choice. This time of year, the safest spot for us is tucked in here." Bill picked up his notebook and motioned for me to go out and back to the galley.

How would I be able to enjoy the rest of our evening and remembrance of the holy night when all I could picture was ice encapsulating the boat?

CHAPTER 23

IN THE EARLY MORNING OF CHRISTMAS DAY, I HEARD Bill shut our door and go to pull the anchor. I lay still and waited for him to be gone before I inched out of bed to take a peek out the galley window. Would there be ice? Perhaps the temperature was warmer than what he'd predicted for last night's low. It was so dark and with the moon behind the clouds it was difficult to see, so I went back to bed and pulled the covers higher up, shielding my face from the cool air. Bill returned after a few short minutes, and I rolled over. "Back so soon?"

"Sorry, I didn't mean to wake you up. Yeah, I'll wait a little longer. The barometric reading is falling, and I want to watch that. Go back to sleep." He grabbed his hat and went back out, shutting the door behind him.

I stared at the wall and pictured Bill camping out in the wheelhouse, making his plans while he sipped coffee. Before our first boat adventure I wouldn't have guessed that fishing would be a twenty-four-hour job at times. Having grown up in the Oregon countryside, I wasn't familiar with the maritime climate or lifestyle. It seemed like all we did was set pots, wait it out, and go back for them, but that was the routine.

I rubbed my feet together to warm them up. Without Bill next to me in bed I was often chilled and needed to add a fleece blanket. I reached for one next to my side of the bed and spread it out. Closing my eyes, I recalled last night when Stanna stayed up late to hide the gifts and create clues suggesting where each person should look so that we wouldn't turn the boat upside down. This day promised more memories.

I lay still for a little longer, considering getting up to make fresh cinnamon rolls like I used to back home. I'd bought all the ingredients with high hopes of making some in the next few weeks. Wouldn't this be the best day to surprise everyone? I rubbed my feet together again, then hopped out of bed to get changed and sneak into the galley. Thankfully, the kids' bunk room was further down the ship, and they rarely woke up to clatter from this end.

In the galley, I pulled the butter out of the fridge to soften while I warmed some milk on the stove. A Christmas hymn came to mind. Clearing my throat, I started to sing.

"What Child is this who laid to rest on Mary's lap is sleeping? Whom angels greet with anthems sweet, while shepherds watch are keeping? This, this is Christ the King, whom shepherds guard and angels sing; haste, haste, to bring Him laud, the Babe, the Son of Mary."

Having grown up going to church, I knew many of the hymns by heart. I didn't have a musical note in my bones and could hardly carry a tune, but I loved to sing along with the crowd. I pictured the beauty of us all worshiping God in Heaven in His presence one day. I continued on with the second verse.

"Why lies He in such mean estate, where ox and ass are feeding? Good Christians, fear, for sinners here, the silent Word is pleading. Nails, spear shall pierce Him through, the cross be borne for me, for you. Hail, hail the Word made flesh, the Babe, the Son of Mary."

I stopped singing to turn off the heat under the pot of milk.

Chapter 23

It had reached the right temperature and needed to cool before I added the first bit of flour and yeast. Baking for the family was something I missed, and I felt like I was preparing a feast by giving them this small token of a memory from years gone by.

It wasn't the food or the traditions but the remembrance of Jesus' birth. I thought back to the birth of each of my five babies and the love that welled up when I first held each of them. I couldn't fathom the loss Mary felt when she saw her son up on the cross, taking on the sins of the world. Jesus was born so that He could die. I put my hand over my heart and stopped. Tears came to my eyes. There it was again—G-R-A-C-E, God's riches at Christ's expense. He died and rose again for me. I closed my eyes and sang the third verse.

"So, bring Him incense, gold and myrrh, come peasant, king to own Him; the King of king's salvation brings, let loving hearts enthrone Him. Raise, raise a song on high, the virgin sings her lullaby. Joy, joy for Christ is born, the Babe, the Son of Mary."

I let the tears flow down my face, and I imagined myself kneeling before the baby lying in a humble manger.

"Thanks be to God for sending His son. Thank You, Jesus, for dying for me, and thank You to the Holy Spirit for living in me so that I can have the promise of a relationship both now and for eternity. Thank You for Christmas when I remember and celebrate my faith in the King of Kings."

I wiped the tears from my eyes and dabbed my hands on my apron. Pulling out the sugar and baking soda, I heard a horrific noise that startled me. I moved over to the window and saw the faint red glow of morning in the cloudy sky. My gaze moved from the dark mountaintop down to the ocean. I squinted to see it clearly and saw the reason for the noise. The dull, opaque sheen was ice, and Bill was raising the anchor.

My heart raced at the sight of it. "*Oh, God, calm my soul.*"

An unfamiliar clattering noise rose from under the boat, and I scrunched my face at the sound. What was happening? I wiped my clammy hands on my apron and held it taut. *Should I run to Bill or assume he has things under control? What do I do? Didn't Bill mention last time that I should run when I hear a loud noise to make sure we hadn't hit a large object like a floating log?*

I put the lid on the pot and cringed as the noise got louder. "Lord, this can't be good. It sounds worse than before."

My conversation with God caught me silly. He knew exactly what was going on. Why was I telling Him? Reaching for my coat, I glanced down the hall to see if any of the kids were getting up. I hurried to the wheelhouse, putting my hands over my ears so the echo wouldn't hurt. The pain of the noise reverberated in my head.

"Bill," I shouted over the noise, "is everything okay?" My words were dampened by the clattering beneath me.

Bill stood next to the controls and jumped as he caught site of me from of the corner of his eye. His ashen face and rapid breathing radiated fear. "The anchor is catching. I don't know if it's that or a gear in the chain locker." He took off his hat and ran his hand through his hair, then put his hat back on.

"The other noise?" I raised my voice as loud as I could. "What is it?"

Looking outside, then back to me, he pointed out and down at the ice coating the ocean. "The ice," he shouted. "Much thicker than last time."

Without thinking, I cried out. "Dear God, keep us safe. Help Bill to know what to do. Please help the anchor work so we can get out of here."

Bill gave me a half-smile and squeezed my hand. "You're cold. Go back in. I'll keep messing with it."

I nodded and walked back to the galley, praying earnestly. *Let us break free, God. Break us free.* I didn't want my fear to paralyze me. Not on Christmas, not ever.

Chapter 23

IN THE GALLEY, I FOUND A PAIR OF EARMUFFS AND PUT them on while I worked to finish the cinnamon rolls. As I placed the rolls in the pan and placed a tea towel over them to rise, the boat jolted and the clattering stopped.

"Ah, thank God, the anchor must have released." I spoke out loud, knowing no one would hear me above the piercing noise of the boat breaking through the ice. I couldn't fathom how the kids slept through it, but perhaps they were too afraid to move. I walked back to the bunk room and peeked in. The boys were huddled on Daniel's bottom bunk, looking at a comic book and the girls were on Rayna's bunk, fixing each other's hair.

"Merry Christmas," I shouted.

The kids looked up and started laughing. "You look hilarious." Rob said, pointing at me.

I'd not considered how silly I would appear with a flour-matted apron and my fuzzy earmuffs. I laughed too.

"What is that noise?" Daniel pointed to the wall.

"Ice." I stated matter-of-factly, hoping they wouldn't see the uneasy tension I held back. "We'll be ready to eat in about an hour." I smiled at them, then returned to the galley.

As I walked past the large window next to the table, the crimson glow in the sky sparked a memory of our first day out in the harbor. The fisherman warned us of the impending storm, their warning written on the horizon. Would it prove true? The scratching sound of the ice lessened, and the hum of the engine took over. I let out a long, deep sigh and went to see Bill.

"Thank God, that's over," I said and put my hand on his shoulder.

"Yah, but that's not the worst of it." He pointed at the barometer and tapped it. "There's a storm coming."

"Not again," I said, before thinking.

"I'll try and get us to a good vantage point where we won't have ice. Don't wait breakfast for me." He kept his gaze set ahead.

"Okay." I let out the breath I was holding. "I'll bring you a cinnamon roll later." I walked back, thankful for God's grace in getting us out of the ice, but also wondering how bad it would get later?

Do not worry. My Grace is sufficient. A part of a Bible verse from the gospel of Matthew came to mind, and I nodded. *Yes, God, it is.*

CHAPTER 24

THE KIDS FOLLOWED THEIR CLUES TO THEIR stockings while I put the egg casserole on the table. I steadied myself, placing the cinnamon rolls next to it as the bobbing of the boat grew with each minute. Clouds moved in from the west and lowered down over the tops of the islands near us.

I thought of Jonah and the task he'd been given to preach repentance to the people of Nineveh. I shook my head, I could relate. Truthfully, I'd have run right along with him to avoid the confrontation. However, after seeing how mightily God worked in those peoples' lives, I saw power in standing firm and not fleeing or hiding in the belly of a whale.

Putting the coffee percolator on the stove top, I hurried to make what I could before we'd have to hunker down from the waves.

The wind whistled, and I rubbed my hands together. A winter storm meant a chill in the boat. I longed for my wood-stove in the corner at home where I could back up to it and then rotate my body.

"Found mine," Laura called out as she set her stocking on the ledge.

"Great," I answered back. "Will you help finish setting the

table? We need to eat and get things put away before this storm gets any worse."

"Sure. It smells great." She walked past me and put napkins on the table.

One by one, the kids came in telling me about their Christmas treasure hunt.

"Rob, will you please pray for the food?" I pulled off my apron.

"Yup. Thank You, God, for sending Your son Jesus and for this amazing food we are about to eat. Amen." He reached for a cinnamon roll at lightning speed.

"Hey, slow it down. We need to save some for your dad." I added, "We should probably pray for safety too, that we can hide away from the storm soon."

"Really?" Stanna asked.

I shrugged my shoulders and looked out at the darkening sky. "I'm guessing once we're in a cove or bay we will be fine, we just need to get there."

"Mm, Mom, these are soooo good." Daniel said with his mouth full of cinnamon roll. I haven't had one in ages."

It was all the thanks I needed for the work that went into preparing the meal early that morning. "You are welcome. Glad you like them." I stood up and poured myself a cup of coffee, noticing the white caps on the waves outside the window. Their height was nearing three to four feet. I'd brewed coffee, but the ocean was brewing a storm with us in the middle of its fury. It was time for me to live out my choice to trust God in the midst of the torrent.

"Let's pray for safety," I said, standing next to the stove. The kids all bowed their heads and closed their eyes before I started. I watched their faces as I began. "God, we ask for Your hand of mercy to get us to safety. Please direct Bill, and help us to remain calm. In Jesus name, Amen."

A round of amens followed mine. I prepared a plate for Bill

and, after I bundled up in my warm coat and put a stocking hat on, took it out to him.

"Just in time," Bill shouted and took the plate from me. He set it on the ledge and grabbed my hands, placing them on the wheel. "Hold it here. I'll be right back." Before I could answer, he headed out the door and into the storm.

Oh great, what could it be now? Scanning the scene on the other side of the window, I couldn't see more than five feet above the water. The dark of the clouds felt like it was nearing evening even though it was barely nine in the morning. I hummed *Jesus Loves Me* to myself, hoping to calm my nerves. We went from one moment of chaos to another. Would I end up a jittery, old lady at the end of all this, having spent every ounce of energy on worry? I inhaled. No, I wouldn't. I would triumph with God's help and be a woman of prayer.

Bill returned and motioned for me to let the wheel go.

"What is it?" I asked and zipped my coat up further.

"It's the blasted anchor. It didn't come up all the way, and I don't think there is anything I can do now." He reached for the plate. "Thanks for the food."

"What can I do?" I rubbed my hands.

Bill moved his gaze from his plate up to me. "This is a change. You haven't been so...eager and perky."

He was right. I'd avoided being his sidekick, making any excuse I could. "If you don't need me now, I can come back," I offered.

He looked at his watch and back to me. "How about you send the boys in an hour."

"Sure." I took his cup. "Only after I bring you more coffee." I darted out before he could protest.

Back in the kitchen, I hurried with my meal so I could clean up. "Girls, will you help me tidy up while the boys go out to Dad?"

"Sure." Stanna answered and stood up. "Thanks again, that

was very good. I guess I should learn to make Grandma's recipe one of these days."

"Yeah, I learned when—"

The engine amped up, and I lost my balance and reached for the counter. "Boys, go now and help your dad."

The darkness hung lower in the sky, reminding me of the looming clouds before a tornado. It made me wish the effects of the storm would slow down so I could process the most efficient way to handle it. As I turned to begin rapid-fire instructions to the girls, I saw they'd already sprung into action, putting breakfast dishes in totes and clearing surfaces.

"Thank you," I called out over the noise of the wind and grabbed my coat. "I'm going to go and—" Cut off by a screeching sound that echoed through the boat, I placed my hands on my ears, squinting my eyes and hoping it wasn't ice or something else tearing into the bottom of the boat.

The engine died, and the boat jerked, tossing me to the floor. Books slid off the counter next to me, and Rayna screamed. I crawled over to where she huddled next to Stanna. "Girls!" I shouted, "we'll get this mess later. Go to your bunks." I gave them a little push, and they hunkered as they walked, shielding their heads as though the ceiling was crashing down around them.

I steadied myself and zipped up my coat as I walked. "God, I hope they're okay." My stomach felt as hard as a rock as I envisioned the boys slipping with the jolt of the boat.

In the wheelhouse, all the guys stood around yelling over the howl of the wind. They braced themselves on the stool and ledges as the boat rose to crest a large wave.

I waited for a break in the conversation to yell, "What's going on?" Searching Bill's face, I saw his damp eyes of concern.

"The anchor let out and won't come back up." He pointed outside. "You can't see it, but we are dangerously close to the beach with the wind pushing us that way. I've got to get out and

Chapter 24

fix it. Boys you come with me, and babe—" He paused and reached for me, holding my shoulders with his strong hands. "I need you. I need you to steer us with the engine on. Watch the fish finder to see our depth, and keep us on course away from rocks. You can do it."

I blinked rapidly and pressed my elbows into my sides. With a shrill voice, I answered, "I can."

The guys scrambled to find tools and their life preservers, which would prove almost useless in a storm like this. As they were about to go out the door, Bill froze, then turned. "Let's pray. God help us, keep us away from danger. Loose the anchor, and help Grace steer us to safety. Amen." Bill's eyes pleaded with mine, and I nodded at him.

I gripped the wheel and turned on the engine, watching the depths below us. I could see the direction I needed to head and fixed my gaze on the compass. Due north would take us straight out, and Bill could take it from there.

Driving us back and forth, from side to side, I felt like time moved in slow motion. "Oh, God, how did I get into this again?" The boat crested a wave, and we came crashing down. "Please, please God, let the guys be safe," I cried out.

"Again, God, again. I need Your word to wash over me," I pleaded into the darkness surrounding me, threatening to crush my spirit. Only divine help would see us through to the end.

Immediately, I was impressed with the words "*God is our refuge and strength, a very present help in trouble.*"

"Yes!" I called out. "Yes, You are." I braced myself as the boat leaned to the side, and I turned the wheel, holding it in place. "More God, more. I'm so alone."

"*But the Lord is faithful, who will establish you, and keep you from evil.*" The verse from Thessalonians was one Amanda had given me. I exhaled deeply, then inhaled. "I will be kept from evil, I will. God, please keep the guys safe," I pleaded with tears welling in my eyes.

The minutes felt like sands in an hourglass the size of a mountain. Would they be able to fix the anchor? How else would we be set free? I jerked the wheel from the force of a wave and watched the depths of the water on the control panel. I couldn't steer long in that direction. I needed to direct us east and then back to the north.

"I need more strength, God. More," I called out and rubbed the tears from my eyes so I could see clearly.

"The name of the Lord is a strong tower, the righteous runneth into it and is safe."

"Jesus! Jesus!" Only You can help us. I gripped the wheel, and my knuckles whitened. "It's You, Jesus."

I cleared my throat and yelled out, "Jesus" and then I whispered, "Jesus."

A peace came over me like I'd never experienced before. It tingled from the base of my neck down my back and the sides of my legs. God was with me. I could feel His presence and the gear knocked on the anchor lever. I looked down at it, questioning whether I should touch it as Bill and the boys walked through the door.

"It's fixed," Bill called out and grabbed the wheel.

I fell into the side of him and closed my eyes. My mighty God had taken us through. "Thank You, Lord," I said and let the tears well up and overflow.

BILL LED US THROUGH STIKINE STRAIT TOWARD Wrangell, and the winds began to die down. By the time we neared Woronkofski Island, the clouds began to dissipate. Red at morn, sailors take warn shook us to the core.

I walked into the wheelhouse with an oversized wool

Chapter 24

sweater over top of my sweatshirt. "Here's the coffee I promised you." I handed a mug of piping hot, black coffee to Bill.

"Took you long enough," Bill joked and pulled me to his side. He kissed the top of my head. "You are my amazing Grace. Today —" He gulped and then sipped his coffee. "I can't tell you enough how much it means to me that you stood by me today."

I flattened my lips in a smile. "Well, you were under attack. What else does a gal do?"

I looked down at my Xtratuff rubber boots that I now wore with pride. "I did a pretty good job of running away like Jonah did, and with a lot of pouting too." I twisted and looked into Bill's eyes. My love for him pulsated through my body. "I want to be here for you. I'm discovering God is here with me, cheering me on and with His help, I can soar like an eagle."

Bill rubbed his jaw. "Even if it means we keep fishing?" He tilted his head to the side and brought his mug up to his lips. "Like, again next year?"

With an acute sense of purpose, I straightened my shoulders. "Yes, because my God can see me through whatever comes my way." I stood on my tip toes and kissed my mighty Alaskan fisherman, hoping he felt my enduring love and determination to serve God alongside him no matter where our adventures took us.

CHAPTER 25

I RUBBED MY HANDS TOGETHER OVER THE FIRE AT Shoemaker Park in Wrangell. We arrived a few nights ago and spent Christmas with Steve and Kim. Today, on New Year's Day, the kids were walking with a group ready to participate in the Polar Plunge—a timed submersion into the Pacific waters here in Shoemaker Bay. I shivered at the thought of the frigid waters, but delighted in their enthusiasm to be a part of it and make memories. Our third season of fishing was profitable enough for us to take some time off and enjoy some of the perks of city life, like swimming at the pool, pizza from the restaurant, and leisurely evenings docked in the harbor.

Leaving the comforts of home in Oregon to follow Bill's passion as a commercial fisherman was more than I'd ever bargained for. For months, I hadn't been sure how to support him in his efforts and find the inner peace I needed in order to allow God to supply my every need. Finding God's grace in every circumstance would be a lifelong lesson, but I was learning to lean on Him instead of escaping through vices that left me empty.

"Hey friend," Annie called out as she walked toward me from the pavilion.

Chapter 25

"Hi. Your kids going out?" I motioned toward the shore.

"Yup, some of them. Yours?" Her contagious smile lit her face.

"They all said they wanted to give it a try." I shuddered and raised my eyebrows.

"Would your family like to come over later and play games?" Annie reached into her coat pocket and pulled out some gloves.

"That sounds great." Memories of our game nights back in Oregon came to mind, as well as the many times we gathered in the galley of the boat or the "basement" to take our minds off the business of fishing.

Annie and I cheered as the announcer called out the countdown for the polar plunge challenge. I turned to watch the kids make their way out into the ocean waters, and I clapped for them. "They're so brave." "They're Alaskans!" Annie turned and faced me. "Brave? I'd say you're the brave one, living on your boat year round."

I shrugged. I'd learned to take it in stride as best I could, knowing God supplied our needs from one moment to the next.

"Your Alaskan life is at a whole different caliber though, my friend. I know I find it a challenge to meal plan for my seven kids, and I live here on the island. How do you juggle that mom job?" Annie tucked some loose strands of hair under her waterproof ball cap.

"We stock up and then make do when we run out of something." I'd learned to keep a running list of items we'd need to buy when we docked on an island with a store.

"What about when someone is sick? Just last week Ally had the worst cough over the weekend and I had to take her to the ER since it was after hours. I can't imagine having to wait until we could coast the waters to find a doctor at the nearest town." She moved closer to the firepit and squatted down.

"Thankfully, the worst scare didn't require immediate attention." I thought back to the event, and my stomach lurched.

"Rob was knocked in the face and got his teeth knocked out from the inside out, and he could stick his tongue out of his cheek." I rolled my eyes. "We made a run to town, and it only took five hours."

"Oh my." Annie stood up. "It's amazing any of us make it to adulthood. But what about your drinking and wash water? And fuel? My dad had a little skiff, and he carried a gallon jug of gas with him in case the little kicker ran out, but with a big boat like yours, I'm sure it's a whole different scenario."

I rubbed my hands over the fire some more, thankful for its warmth and the time on land. "Both the water and fuel tanks are very big, and we've not had any issues. You have such great questions." I smiled at her and raised my eyebrows as Bill's hands gripped my shoulders and gave them a squeeze. "Hey there." I leaned back against him.

"Hi. And hey there, Annie. How's Kyle?" Bill massaged my neck and tucked my scarf back in around the back of my neck.

"Doing good. He'll be excited to see you when you come this evening. Oh, gotta go." Annie waved and rushed with a towel over to one of her younger boys.

"They invited us to go play games. Does that work?" I searched Bill's face, certain he'd agree.

The past fall, our fishing success meant more downtime, less stress, and more opportunity for family fun, especially with Stanna back from college for winter break.

"I'd like that." Bill stepped away from me and closer to the fire. "When the kids are warmed up, how would you like to go for a drive?"

I crouched closer to the fire. "I'd like that." Smiling, I watched Bill's face soften when his eyes met mine. We were thriving, us and the kids. Life was falling into a rhythm and there was much to be thankful for.

WE DROVE THE ROAD TO THE END OF THE PAVEMENT, around twelve miles out of town, then turned the truck around and headed back to the main part of town. A couple of the older kids had gone home with Annie, and the three younger ones were visiting in the back seat, revisiting their excitement from the New Year's party the night before and then the plunge from that afternoon.

I laid my head back on the head rest and watched the ocean from the window. My outlook on the ocean and the maritime climate morphed into an appreciation for the beauty of the Alaskan sea. All year long the ocean was alive, and there was a never-ending view of the mountains surrounding the area.

Bill turned down the road past the school, and I continued to watch out the window, thinking of how nice it was to take a short drive. We pulled into the airport, and I looked over at Bill. "What are we doing here?"

"I had a package sent on the milk run out of Seattle." He let the truck run and undid his seat belt. "Be right back."

I shrugged, not sure what it could be. After digging in my purse for my ChapStick, I pulled out some snacks I'd placed in there earlier. "Here." I turned in my seat to hand them to the kids.

"Thanks—Grandma?" Rayna said.

"Grandma? I'm not Grandma." I laughed and reached to tickle her knee.

"No." She pointed out the window. "It's Grandma."

Twisting in my seat, I darted my gaze out the window. There was my mom walking with Bill, waving and laughing.

I opened my door and ran to her with tears in my eyes. "Momma!"

Amanda came through the door behind them, pulling a suitcase. I reached out to my mom and hugged her tight, inhaling the familiar and invigorating floral smell of the perfume she always wore. "Momma."

"Grandma!" The kids called out and joined us in a hug outside the terminal doors.

"How'd you get in the middle?" I questioned Amanda as we exchanged a long hug.

She brushed her gray curls from her face and tucked them behind her ear. "I wouldn't have missed this moment for the world. I've been meaning to come up for a visit, and when Bill mentioned helping to get your mom to the airport, I volunteered to come along with her all the way here!"

I looked around to see Bill beaming as he watched the commotion. He took the suitcase from Amanda and led the way back to the truck.

"Looks like y'all are right at home here. I can't wait to see your ship." My mom winked at me, then tousled Daniel's hair. "I hope you're ready for some late nights and lots of UNO."

Bill helped my mom into the truck, shut the door, and turned to help me get in on my side. I grabbed his hand and pulled it close to my neck. "Thank you."

He leaned down and kissed me gently. "No, Grace, it's *you* I need to praise for all the sacrifices you've made to move the family, adjust to our new life, and support me. I asked a lot. The least I could do was bring your mom up for a visit."

Heat rose to my cheeks, and a wide smile spread across my face. I was so proud of my Alaskan man, the dreams he had for our whole family, and how he saw it play out over time.

Mom's window rolled down. "Are you going to smooch all day, or can I see that canoe of yours?"

We threw our heads back in laughter at her animated and outgoing ways, which were more hilarious each year.

As we rode over to the other side of the island, I appreciated our Alaskan life that we'd made and the adventures that drew us to grow in our walk with the Lord. The unique challenges were our spiritual inspiration. God's riches at Christ's expense were evident in our lives.

Thank You, Lord, for my life here and letting the escape I longed for bring me to who I am in Christ today. Blessed.

EPILOGUE

We'd left Haines Junction, a small town in the territory Yukon, Canada, about two hours ago. I looked out my window at Kluane Lake, which we skirted as we drove on the Alaska Highway. Not more than another hour and we'd cross the Canadian-American border and head for our new winter home in Tok, Alaska.

The first leg of our trip began two days ago, traveling on the Alaska Marine Highway by ferry from Wrangell to Haines, which was about twenty hours. After spending the night in Haines, we began the eight-hour drive through a tiny portion of British Columbia, followed by the Yukon and onto Alaska.

Out of Haines, the road wound alongside the steep valley, and we left the proud trees of Southeast Alaska behind us. Earlier, the bald eagle sanctuary reminded me of the years of soaring on eagle's wings as a Christian, facing the many challenges to my faith as a mom and wife. I'd learned so much about knitting proper habits to care for my soul those fifteen years we lived on the boat, I'd nestled in next to Bill and stood by his side with my shield of faith and sword of the Spirit.

For the last few years, Rayna and Bill had traveled north on a fall hunt out of Tok. Between crabbing and shrimping seasons, they'd flown commercially to Anchorage, rented a car, and hired a transporter from Tok to fly them out to an area called Forty-Mile Country, where they camped on the tundra and hunted caribou. Rayna took a liking to one of the bush pilots who flew them to the remote hunting spot. Now that she was married to him with a family of her own, we'd been up to visit a few times, enjoying the slower pace and friendly people of the small town.

While on a trip last winter, Bill and I went for a walk in the snow and he paused and took my hand. He knelt down in front of me. "My amazing Grace. After living on the boat for many years, will you recommit your life with me and spend the winters in Tok in a log cabin?"

"What?" I felt my hands start to shake. Was he serious, or was this a joke? I was certain we'd die of old age on our boat. He was my fearless fisherman.

"I'm for real. I see how much you love it here, and I don't see why we can't stay in the winter and then travel down to fish during the summer. Why don't you pick out a log house you love, and we'll set up a home."

"You really are serious." I pulled at his hand for him to stand up. I wrapped my arms around him as best as I could with my large parka and his down-filled coat between us. "Yes, yes, please."

It hadn't taken us long to find a cabin we adored: a three-bedroom with a loft space that nestled over half the house, all on five acres of land. It would work perfectly for grandkids when they came for overnight visits or up from the lower forty-eight states. There was also a garage for storage and a chicken coop out back. I couldn't wait to put logs in a woodstove and knit by the warm fire with my slippered feet tucked under me.

"It's still surreal that we're moving up here," I said and picked up my travel cup to sip my hot coffee.

"I know. Who would have ever guessed we'd go back to our log-cabin life, except this time, it's not in Oregon, but the interior of Alaska on a cold November afternoon." Bill tapped on the dash.

"Why do you keep doing that?" I questioned as I pulled out a skein of yarn from the bag by my feet.

"Don't you hear that whine?" He tapped it again.

"Now that you mention it, I do." I wound the yarn around my knitting needle and counted the stitches I was casting on.

"I'll slow down a bit and see if it gets any better." The truck slowed and Bill pulled over closer to the edge of the lane.

The ALCAN highway was quiet. I assumed that this time of year, there wasn't much traffic on the road, which usually saw thousands of tourists in the summer months. When we'd stopped in the small town of Haines Junction, the people we met were friendly and had mentioned one last place we could stop at between there and Beaver Creek before the border into Alaska. We'd stopped at that last fuel stop and used the bathroom. Anxious to drive in the daylight, we didn't linger to look in the gift shop or stop for a meal, but jumped back into the truck for the last remote stretch of highway. After that fuel stop, we wouldn't need to stop again, not with Tok only ninety miles from the Canadian-American border crossing.

The whine lessened, and Bill slowed the vehicle.

"What are you going to do? Drive fifteen miles an hour the rest of the way?" I was teasing but was also curious as to whether that might become the plan.

I zipped my coat up and shivered. Was it getting colder?

"Shoot, I don't know what the deal is," Bill stated as he gave the steering wheel a light smack.

"And?"

"And, it can't be good. We can hope that we can keep plugging along for as long as we can." Bill reached out to turn on the stereo.

"I've certainly experienced the truth of plugging along as

long as we can after all these years. One mile at a time, babe." I placed my hand on his and gave it a little squeeze.

Bill returned the squeeze and turned the stereo to the story we'd been listening to.

We drove slower and inched alongside the road. While we listened, memories of our family life out on the boat came rushing back at me like a winter wind off the Stikine River. One season of fishing turned into fifteen years of living on the boat. One by one, our kids had graduated and moved on. Three of them were in Oregon, one was in Wrangell, and the baby of the family was in Tok. For years, I'd pined over buying a house in Wrangell, but it'd never come to fruition. We were the fishing crew that sprang from one opener to the next. Perhaps God smiled down at me, knowing a more suitable fit for us was to be nestled in the Arctic desert of the Tanana Valley in Tok. I was sure I'd miss the ocean at times, but returning to our cabin life warmed me from the inside out. There were bike paths I could ride, and a nice little Bible church I'd visited would become my new church family.

The lonely highway stretched out before us. After a few minutes, I spoke over the story. "I know those Canadians are real friendly; maybe we should put our hazards on, and if a vehicle comes by we can ask for help."

The whine increased and pierced my ears, reminding me of the times we'd broken through freshwater ice on the ocean. I placed my hands over my ears, and our truck stopped abruptly. "What in the world?" I held onto the dash.

Bill turned the key to shut down the already-dead engine. "I guess we're stopping."

"Oh, okay." What could I say?

The snow was untouched, and this part of the Yukon Territory was barren of civilization. We hadn't seen another vehicle since we'd left the last stop almost an hour ago.

We sat in silence, and Bill rubbed his temples. "I'll see if it'll start." He turned the key, and the engine turned over. "Good, we can let it run a bit and at least turn on the heater, but I'm afraid we won't be able to move."

"Are you for real?" I didn't doubt him, but I didn't want to swallow the reality of how dangerous the situation was.

"For real, you and me. You've always wanted these wide-open spaces on land. Now you have it." He smiled and spread his arms out.

I hit him in the arm. "Funny. You know I didn't mean it like that."

"No, no, you do. You like peace and quiet. It's very quiet here." He teased me more, and I pinched his knee.

"Set your watch because we can't do this for long or we'll run out of gas." Bill pointed at my wrist.

Another fact I didn't want to linger on. If we didn't have gas, then we didn't have heat.

"I know. I have that quilt that Amanda gave me. I can get it out." I reached behind me and pulled out the beautiful teal and cream quilt she'd made me as a going-away gift. She'd given it to me when we'd traveled down to Oregon to say our goodbyes and pick up the household goods we'd kept in storage for years. As I pulled it out, I ran my hand down the underside. "Oh, thank God she felt inspired to make the back of it flannel." I stretched it out and covered my legs, then held it out, offering Bill the other half.

"Thanks." He tucked his side in over his leg and near the door.

After a few minutes, my watch beeped, and Bill turned off the vehicle. It didn't take long for the below-zero temps to overtake the truck. I started to see my own breath, and a chill went down my back.

"I have some of my homemade trail mix that I packed for the road. Maybe a little snack will help take our mind off things." I pulled out the brown paper sacks from my tote and handed one to Bill.

The three by five card on the side of the bag caught my attention. When I'd packed them, I'd been writing out the verse to memorize the Psalm from chapter 121. Instead of writing trail mix I'd taped the verse to the bag. "Huh, isn't that perfect."

"What?" Bill peered into the bag.

"Look at the verse I put on. 'I lift my eyes up to the mountains—where does my help come from? My help comes from You, Maker of heaven, Creator of the earth.' Just what we need right now, a reminder our help comes from Him."

Bill chewed on some almonds, then paused. "It certainly does."

"Oh, hey, I almost forgot. Amanda gave me a small, little candle too. Can we burn that in here to help keep us warm?"

"Yep, I'll just put my window down a sliver." Bill cranked down his window of the old truck.

I reached back into the bag and pulled out the candle. After years of living on the boat, I usually carried a lighter with me, but I'd purposely thrown the empty one from my purse in the garbage and not bothered to buy a new one. "Hmm, can you pass me the cigarette lighter from the dash, and I'll try and light this tissue." I pulled the remnants of a travel pack of Kleenex and bunched it up in my fingers.

Bill tugged the lighter out and placed it against the tissue. Nothing happened. I watched his face as he put the lighter back into its place and counted out loud for a few seconds before trying again. "C'mon, c'mon," I chanted.

A smolder began to burn. He quickly moved it to the candle, and the wick caught the flame.

"Phew, thank God. I'd say Amanda must have been listening to whispers of the Lord when she thought to gift you with those. We might be here for a while." Bill placed the small candle on the dash and rubbed his hands together before tucking them under the blanket.

We saw some lights coming toward us. "Right on," I said and rolled up my window that I'd also rolled down a smidge. The vehicle drove right on past us.

"What!" I called out. "You've got to be kidding me. Why wouldn't they stop?"

Bill kept his thoughts to himself and started the rig again while I set my timer. "I can hardly believe it. I figured I would have died a tragic death on the boat numerous times, and now we're going to freeze to death, stranded in the Canadian arctic." I let out a sigh and then chuckled. "I really thought I'd meet my maker more than once already in those storms out at sea."

"Amazing Grace, how soon you forget." Bill spoke barely over a whisper. "That it's not the trial or the tempest but it's—"

I finished the sentence for him. "God's riches at Christ's expense." I knew the acronym. I'd preached it repeatedly to my kids after the storm on Christmas that first year. It had come to be the root of my namesake and my lifeline. "Next, you're going to tell me, He's in it all. Seeing us through to the end. Always. His riches abound even now."

"I couldn't have said it better myself," Bill said with a shiver in his voice. The light in the sky was growing fainter now that the sun dipped below the mountain range to the south even though it was barely past noon. "We have the quilt from Amanda and the candle. God is going to provide."

I shuffled closer to him and pulled the blanket up higher around his chest. "I was hoping for more cuddle time this winter, but this is not quite what I imagined."

Bill put his arm around my shoulders. "Dear Heavenly Father, I pray that you provide a way of escape for us. Thank you for the warm blanket and the heat from the candle. In the mighty name of Jesus. Amen."

"Amen." I echoed him and curled my legs underneath me.

"I'll turn the engine on again for just a little bit, but I want to conserve the gas if we have to do this into the night." Bill turned the key, and we put our hands close to the vents. The engine was cooling off, so it wasn't producing much heat anymore.

"You'd think there would be at least someone on the road before it gets to be evening. I don't want to think about being out here at night." I pictured our hazards as they stopped flashing and our blacked-out truck on the side of the road as it was hit from the behind by a semi.

"How about we talk about something else. Tell me one thing you're looking forward to at our new place." Bill kissed the top of my head.

"A bigger bed." I didn't have to think long. I knew I would savor every inch of our house, but I was looking forward to enjoying the grandiose space of a king-sized mattress.

Bill chuckled. "I'm looking forward to having a garage where I can tinker on things. This is going to be a great semi-retirement. For both of us."

"Indeed," I agreed.

The jake break of a truck hammered in my ears, and I pushed against Bill to see out his window. A semi was slowing down behind us. "Oh, thank You, Lord."

The trucker stopped ahead of us, and a man climbed out of his truck and walked to us. Bill stepped out to explain, then re-opened his door. "Get what you need for the night. He can get us to the town of Beaver Creek where we can call Rayna. Then they can come help us with the truck tomorrow."

Thank you, Jesus, thank you! The prayer came out. *You've made the way of escape. You see it through to the end.*

WAIT...before you go will you do me a favor? Will you take the time to write a review for me on the Goodreads? Just a few words of how the story resonated with you.

https://www.goodreads.com/book/show/61933012-alaskan-escape

Also head on over to my website at *https://www.mary-ann-landers.com and subscribe to my newsletter to stay in the loop.*

ACKNOWLEDGMENTS

When I interviewed a friend about her story it became clear I needed a sermon to help develop the plot line. I'd like to thank *Tim Miles* of Southland Bible Church. God used two of his sermons spaced out over five months to help me understand the Biblical messages that would intertwine Alaskan Escape.

Here is a link to one of the messages:

Jonah: God's Object Lesson, Jonah 4:5-11

As always I'd like to thank my husband, children and extended family for their patience and support.

P.S. It's awfully sweet that my oldest son carries a copy of my first book, Alaskan Calibration around in his backpack at college. Some of life's sweetest compliments are silent gestures.

ABOUT THE AUTHOR

Alaskan based author Maryann Landers writes women's faith filled fiction based on true stories of extraordinary women of her magnificent state. She loves to showcase the unique north and give her readers a little taste of rustic Alaska.

While writing in her log home in the woods she is also looking forward to her next adventure with her Alaskan husband, juggling mom tasks such as crafting homemade meals from moose and caribou meat, building DIY projects from scrap wood piles and guiding her teens in their homeschooling.

To learn about her inspiration to write Alaskan based stories read her blog at www.mary-ann-landers.com

facebook.com/MaryannLandersAUTHOR

ALSO BY MARYANN LANDERS

Book 1 Alaskan Calibration
Book 2 Alaska Calling
Book 3 Alaska Chance

Made in the USA
Middletown, DE
15 October 2022